"IT'S A FILLY!"

It lay there, wet and silent and shining, in the dim circle of light cast by the kerosene lantern. Belle snatched up some rags and began to try to rub some life into the foal's motionless limbs.

"Sure looks poorly to me," she said. "Poor winter babe—I think the hard birth might've been too much for her."

The mare, too weak to get to her feet, called urgently to the foal she could not see. There was no answer from the damp bundle Belle labored over. The mare called again. Again. Each time there was a wilder note of grief in her cry. But suddenly, in a crazy, mixed-up flurry of straw and rags and four long legs that went in every direction at once, the foal stood up.

We stared. In the amber circle of light, that newborn filly gleamed as pale and silvery as a phantom. She was a little never-was right out of some tale told in the Tennessee pinewoods when the moon was full . . .

THE SNOWBIRD

The Latest Books from SIGNET VISTA

THE
SNOWBIRD

BY
PATRICIA CALVERT

A SIGNET VISTA BOOK
NEW AMERICAN LIBRARY
TIMES MIRROR

NAL BOOKS ARE AVAILABLE AT QUANTITY DISCOUNTS WHEN USED TO PROMOTE PRODUCTS OR SERVICES. FOR INFORMATION PLEASE WRITE TO PREMIUM MARKETING DIVISION, THE NEW AMERICAN LIBRARY, INC., 1633 BROADWAY, NEW YORK, NEW YORK 10019.

The Snowbird was written with the assistance of a 1978 work-in-progress award from The Society of Children's Book Writers.

The author wishes to thank *The Friend* (Salt Lake City, Utah), in whose pages a version of *The Snowbird* appeared as a three-part serial in 1977.

RL 4/IL 5+

For
those who know that the white horse
is called by many names,
and one of them is
Hope.

Foreword

White horses occupy a special niche in the recorded facts and fables of human history. . . .

Napoleon mounted his favorite white stallion, *Marengo,* to command the Battle of Waterloo. Later, the horse accompanied its master into exile on the Isle of Elba. Lawrence of Arabia rode a white charger, as did Joan of Arc, and Lady Godiva perched upon a white horse to make her famous tax-protesting ride through the streets of Coventry in the eleventh century. *White Surrey* was the favorite mount of King Richard III, and Buddha called his white stallion *Lampon,* or "shining like a lamp."

Winged, white *Pegasus* carried thunder and lightning for Zeus; Cinderella rode to meet her handsome prince in a coach drawn by six silver horses; the prophet Mahomet ascended into heaven on a silver steed named *Al Borak,* whose coat was "glossy as marble" and whose "tail brushed the ground." According to a Norse legend, the moon is pulled across the sky by a milk-white mare named *Alsvider,* meaning "all-swift," and at the Siege of Antioch a Turk named Pyrrhus saw an army of soldiers mounted on white horses descend from the sky to fight by the side of the Christians.

For centuries, the white-capped waves on lakes around Killarney have been called "O'Donoghue's white horses," in memory of the slain Irish folk hero, and King Alfred ordered the image of a white horse to be carved into the chalk hills of Uffington to commemorate his victory over the Danes in 871 A.D.—a symbol that, on a fair English morning, can still be seen from a distance of twelve miles. To dream of a white horse is always lucky; the Kiowa Indians believed a warrior was invincible in battle when mounted on a white horse; in India, a white horse is the symbol of courage, wisdom, and hope. . . .

1

"The nightmare is almost over," I told myself. *Over, over, over*. The words hummed in my ears like a song. "Those two troublemakers are finally leaving Tipton. When they are gone, you'll be just what you're supposed to be—thirteen, thinner than a pine slat . . . and free!"

For three long months my heart had lain in my chest as cold and round and hard as the turtle I caught once and kept at the bottom of a glass jar; now it began to stir and stretch. Eagerly, I scooped a nest out of the fallen leaves that covered the Widow Wilson's hillside.

It was the perfect place from which to watch the drama unfold on the ribbon of red clay road below—for there, in a carriage driven by Mr. Rich, a girl and a small, light-haired boy had commenced their journey to the railroad station a mile away.

The girl sat ramrod-straight on the leather-covered wagon bench, as if a befuddled Creator had fashioned a poker for her spine. Her right hand gripped the hand of the boy beside her; with the fingers of her left, she ticked off the passing minutes on the painted yellow wheel of Mr. Rich's buggy.

"Crazy," I marveled out loud to the widow's trees. "She is just plain old cat-crazy!"

How else to account for the hat that girl was wearing? I recognized it right off, and so would everyone else in Tipton County. It was made of straw, was decorated with faded paper roses, and had appeared every Sunday for twenty years on the bent gray head of Mrs.

1

Rich as she sat in the front pew of the Tipton County Baptist Church. But it could not hide the peculiar condition of its present wearer's hair.

Poor critter, I thought. *She'd a done herself a favor to've left town brassy and bareheaded. What she did was a crime even a conjure-woman couldn't hide!*

The passengers in the maroon and yellow carriage slipped under my nose, grew smaller and smaller, were transformed into figures you might expect to see through the wrong end of a telescope. Only then did I admit what their passing had done to me: I'd become a stranger inside my own skin. Parts of me had gotten disconnected from other parts. Heart from head. Liver from spleen. Limbs from lanky carcass.

"It's probably on account of *her*." I took to the notion like a pig to a puddle. "She is like . . . like a person from a dream hard to call to mind. Makes me think of one of Beth Ellen's puppets. That little boy, too—both of 'em so stiff and make-believe. . . ."

Ah. That was it.

Those three in the buggy were characters out of another yarn I'd invented. Didn't I do it all the time, until I'd driven my mother to distraction? Why, I knew people who didn't exist better than I knew the members of my own family! I gave those people—the ones who lived in stories I aimed to write someday—a time present and a time future, colored their eyes blue or green or brown, and invested their souls with passions and prejudices as were reflections of my own.

"Figments," Mama had called them, not unkindly. "Figments of an overactive imagination."

I chewed on my lower lip until it began to ooze. The bright taste of my own blood restored me to myself. I had been doing once again what I'd done all summer long: I was still trying to hold fate an arm's length away. *My nightmare was not over.* It might never be.

For that girl on the ribbon of red clay road was not a dream person. Not a figment, either, and surely ought to be no stranger to me. Nor was I a spectator, hunkered on a pair of bony shins in the autumn gloom of a poor widow's woods, spying on three travelers through the wrong end of a telescope. I was observer and observed. Writer and reader. Inventor and invention. *That girl was me. . . .*

Me: a girl who'd been witness to mayhem and murder. Who'd worn a boy's name longer than she liked to remember. A girl descended from James Robertson, who had crossed the Cumberland on Christmas Day, 1779. A girl whose kinswoman, Pauline Cushman, had dared to wear the uniform of a Union major during the Civil War.

But on October 25, 1883, it was me who was accountable—for myself and for a brother who was barely six years old, whose pale hair our dead mother had likened to milkweed down. I was accountable for a life I had not chosen but in whose pursuit I would discover that I was, like my ancestors before me, a dreamer and a teller.

2

I gripped TJ's hand with mine and our sweaty fingers lay in my lap like a tangle of eels. Sure as sin I knew one thing: If there'd been a better way to reach the railroad station, even pursed and pious Mr. Rich would've sought it out. If not for the sake of TJ and me, then for his own. But on that blue and gold October morning there was only one way to reach the Tipton County railway station and only one way to leave it—by traveling the cemetery road.

"Never look back. Put the past behind. That's where it belongs." It was advice I parceled out to TJ until he should've known it by heart. It was not advice I always followed myself. So, knowing it was our last morning in Tennessee and suspecting that never in this life would I travel down that particular stretch of red clay road again, I permitted myself a backward glance.

Beyond the iron fence embracing the Queen of Angels cemetery, tattered scraps of mist were snagged like ladies' veils in the branches of elm and oak and butternut. Dewdrops clung like tears (ones I still refused to shed?) from the tips of spirea and dogwood and honeysuckle. And there, ringed round by all the Bannermans who'd gone before, lay my mother and my father.

WILLIAM AND ANNA BANNERMAN,

DIED BY FIRE, 1883;

AS THEY ARE TODAY,

PREPARE YOURSELVES SOMEDAY TO BE.

I had composed their epitaph myself, but on that final morning the warning I caused to be immortalized on a slab of pink marble did not bring me its usual righteous comfort. Nor did I feel my customary rage at Wash McDermott—rage I'd worn until it felt like a coat made especially for me—for putting my parents in their early graves. Even the fate of the three men in the Tipton County jail, who were accused of carrying out the actual murder, no longer concerned me.

When I am gone from Tipton, I wondered instead, *will anyone in these parts recollect that once upon a time William and Anna Bannerman joined their two ordinary names to make an uncommon one for their only daughter?*

Willanna.

Lordy, Lordy! Wasn't it a name fit to call up visions of ribbons and ruffles and yards of lace? Of course it was! A name as graceful and girlish as any ever invented by two loving parents. But it was about as much like me as a toad is like a turnip. There surely must've been something peculiar in my nature that, having been christened Willanna, I came to be called Willie. Now the name fit. Most of the time I even felt like a Willie.

No doubt it is because I am a too-serious person with eyes the color of old putty, I concluded long ago. *Somehow I am always out of step. Marching left when everyone else is marching right. Always up my own tree, alone.* Papa used to say such a nature was a blessing. Just how, he never bothered to tell me.

My preoccupations triggered an alarm in Mr. Rich, for he harrumphed to me, in that voice Papa said belonged perfectly to a banker ("As soothing to raw nerves, Willie, as a pocketful of money"), "Your parents, God rest their souls, are going to sleep easier knowing you and Thomas Jefferson are finally on your way to the Territory to make a new home with your papa's own dear brother."

Mightily, too, did I yearn to be comforted: *Papa's own dear brother.* I squinched my eyes shut as I'd already done a dozen times before and tried to conjure up a picture of my uncle. But no matter how hard I tried or how long I conjured, no image of a man who looked as dear and kind and tired as Papa presented itself on the dark screen of my closed lids.

"I always considered that Randall Bannerman was a gentleman and a scholar, just like your papa," Mr. Rich droned on. He paused, pulled on his long lower lip—and dropped the other shoe.

"And your Aunt Belle? Well, you and your brother must bear in mind I hardly knew the woman. It was a mystery, I admit it was, to everyone in Tipton how it was she came to marry a man like your uncle. She was a most unusual woman. Everyone agreed on that. A most unusual woman . . ."

My squinched eyes flew open like two roller shades sna-a-a-a-p-ping to the top of the sash. I fastened Mr. Rich with the most baleful glare that I could muster up on such brief notice.

"What's that supposed to mean, Mr. Rich?" I yelled. Mama always claimed I had a short fuse and called me Lady Jane Sapphira-Jones. Now I aimed to do fearsome justice to that assessment of my character.

"You had just better explain that remark, Mr. Rich," I screeched, warming to the challenge. "You fixing for some reason to scare me and my poor orphan brother right out of our wits? And with us about to board that train and leave Tennessee forever to take up Lord knows what kind of a life? What's *wrong* with our Aunt Belle? *Huh,* Mr. Rich? You going to *answer* me, Mr. Rich?"

Fiendish wishes possessed me. To grab onto that rich man and shake him until those tiny brown eyes rolled back in his fat head like two marbles on a tipped plate. To sink my teeth into the pink shank of unbaked ham that was his wrist. To trounce him into the dust of the road like Beth Ellen and I trounced puffballs every spring in the widow's pale green woods. Except it was too late.

The train was waiting for us. Oily and embarrassed, Mr. Rich had but one matter on his mind by that time: to be shut of me and my brother. We were reminders.

He wanted us out of his hair, out of his big white house on Tipton Hill, wanted us safely on our way to Dakota Territory.

Just the same, he had to have the last word. "It wasn't really murder," he cried in my ear. "What happened to your mama and your papa was an accident. Them boys didn't mean to kill your folks! That fire was only a warning, to get your papa to stop the investigation. Don't leave Tipton thinking it was murder!"

I fixed him with my deadliest glance. It was a look I'd practiced twice a day for three months in the hall mirror of his very own house. "I know what I know," I hissed, "and there's some chickens that'll be home to roost someday. Just see if they don't!" I said the words only because they came quickly to mind. I did not really know anything sinister or important. But their effect on Mr. Rich was immediate and telling. He backed away as though I'd delivered a blow to his brisket.

I turned to clamber up the wooden steps of the train, gave TJ a hefty boost with one knee as I did so, and let Papa's old valise bang smartly against my other shin. As soon as we were settled, TJ spit on the heel of his hand and scrubbed a peephole in the dust of the train window. I leaned over and peered out with him.

Mr. Rich, head bent, was beating a hasty retreat up Tipton Hill to the polished halls of his big white house. What was he thinking? That I would return someday, seeking vengeance? I hoped so. Closer by, we could see the weathered station house in whose waiting rooms not so long ago we had played hide-and-seek. Beyond it all was the corner of the red brick jail that housed the three men accused of setting the blaze that took our parents' lives. *Hadn't meant to kill them, Mr. Rich?* Well, I knew what I knew.

The train creaked. Shuddered. Crept forward. TJ flung himself back in his seat so hard he raised up mushrooms of dust at the tip of each skinny shoulder. His eyes, ordinarily the color of crushed violets, were black with terror.

"I ain't ready to go yet, Willie," he whispered. "Maybe tomorrow I'll be ready. But not now. Make somebody stop this here train, Willie. I changed my mind, yes'm, I surely have. I ain't going to the Territory with you after all."

"You don't have any choice in the matter," I said. I grabbed him and hugged him to me tighter than a tick hugs a hound. Not that I loved him all that much. Sometimes I wondered if I loved him at all. To be accountable, after all, is not the same as to love. My motives were strictly practical: to make sure that he did not take a notion to swing like an organ grinder's monkey from the emergency cord or holler for the conductor.

I clapped his face into the folds of my green jacket. "Don't fret, Bubba," I crooned into his milkweed thatch, using Mama's old endearment. "Things are going to be all right, truly they are. We are not going to miss a place called Tennessee at all. Naw. Why, Aunt and Uncle are going to have a pony cart painted green that we can ride in every Sunday afternoon. They'll live in a white house with chinaberry trees all around, and the flowers in the yard will be as big as my head."

Lies, lies, lies. Stitched and patched and pieced together into a seven-color comfort quilt. TJ's tearful hiccups finally subsided. When it seemed to me that he was soothed, I settled back into my own seat and reached into my pocket. I fished out the stub of a pencil and a scrap of paper and made a desk of my bent-up knees. I began to write.

I have been a witness to mayhem and murder and I have worn a boy's name longer than I like to remember. But I am descended from James Robertson, and my kinswoman, Pauline Cushman, once wore the uniform of a Union major. . . .

"Aw, Willie," TJ snuffled piteously, "don't start up that dumb danged writing business again. I can't stand for you to do that no more, Willie. You hear me?" He poked at my bruised shin with his toe.

"TJ, we have fished in this pond before. Like I told you: I got to do what I got to do."

"Why you so set on writing a book, Willie? I'm only six years old. I don't even know how to read."

"You'll learn eventually."

"If I ain't old enough to read your dopey book, Willie Bannerman, you sure ain't old enough to write it," he insisted. "You got to know a whole lot of words to write a book. I mean, a real one, not one of them pretend kind you was always writing when you was supposed to be helping Papa at the *Tribune.* You and that silly office behind the boiler. Orange crate for a desk. What'd you write about? Men and ladies in love? You ain't a lady. Not to mention the fact you don't know a thing about love."

Knew nothing about love? Hadn't I loved Wash McDermott to distraction, ugly and unsuitable as he was and older than Papa to boot, the very Wash whose moustache had been a confabulation of curly red wires and who, it turned out, conspired to murder my own parents?

"You are a needle artist, TJ. Anyone ever tell you that?"

"Be nice to me. I'm an orphan."

"Makes two of us."

"You don't count. You're older'n me. Only not old enough yet to write a real book."

Now it was my opinion that TJ was spoiled when he was born. Perhaps something had gone wrong in his making. It was not a condition that came about just because he got to be an orphan. But Mama had certainly thought TJ was special. Was it because he looked like an elf we'd rescued one twilight from underneath the lilac bush in our front yard the summer I was seven? Or did he in truth possess some rare, insightful gift? Hadn't he, for instance, this moment pressed a rude finger to my tenderest nerve? *How old is old enough?*

"Am too," I assured him sweetly. I would never admit doubt to him. Never. "Besides, I am not writing this book purely for myself. Or for you. I am writing it for Mama and Papa. Papa said dreams don't have to die. Not so long as there's a dreamer left to do the dreaming and a teller left to do the telling. I aim to be both: dreamer and teller. Might even get to be famous someday. Like that Louisa May Alcott I was telling you about. Mama and Papa would be so proud."

Lou-ezza Who-ezza!" TJ snorted. He screwed up his eyes and a pair of tiny white pinch marks showed up on either side of his nose. Altogether, what with his white hair and pale face, he put me in mind of a very mean albino mouse.

"How in the world can Mama and Papa be proud of you, Willie?" he demanded to know. "They ain't going to know one blame thing about your crazy notions. Mama and Papa are dead."

Perhaps until that moment he had never admitted it to himself, for he repeated the word in the most despairing voice it'd ever been my misfortune to hear: "Dead. Dead. Dead." I could actually see it dangling in the air between us, suspended on a gossamer thread, a spider of a word with glittery orbs and tufts of stiff black hair all over: *Dead*.

I reached out to place my two hands on TJ's knees. They were as small and hard and perfect beneath my palms as the knobs that decorated my metal bedstead, melted to a terrible tangle three months ago. "Don't dwell on it," I said. "Anyways, don't you recollect what Papa told us about our name?"

"You are the one with the weird name, Willie. Not me."

"How back there in the olden golden days of England the man who carried the king's colors into battle was called the banner man? And how after that man had a son who carried the king's colors, too, and his son had a son who did the same, how for all time after the whole family was called Bannerman? Remember what Papa said, TJ?"

I peered at him. He had closed his eyes. They were puddled underneath with lavender. I wiggled out of my green jacket and laid it across him. It did not matter whether his sleep was real or feigned. He was courting aloneness and I would let him.

For one thing, it gave me an opportunity to assess our situation. To wit: Our inheritance was packed into Papa's valise that now rested on a rack over our heads.

It contained a mirror with a broken handle, two books (one of them smoke-damaged), and a dress of periwinkle blue that had belonged to Mama. It harbored, in addition, hundreds of bits and pieces and scraps of paper—corners of envelopes, bits of newsprint, backs of old bills of lading—on which I had scribbled my endless tales of love and loss. Such was the sum total of our lives, TJ's and mine, after the fire.

I stared out the window at my side. From that dusty pane a narrow-eyed bandit with abbreviated hair peered back at me. Even now, such a long time later and able to understand many peculiar things, I still cannot explain why I did it.

An hour before my parents' funeral, I had snipped off all my lovely long brown hair with Mrs. Rich's gold embroidery scissors. The scissors were small and my hair was thick, and when I was finished my former pride and glory looked not so much as though it had been cut, but as if it had been chewed off by a ravenous animal with a peculiar appetite.

"Such a pity!" Mrs. Rich had been quick to agree. "Especially for a girl whose only decent feature was a headful of pretty brown hair." I had raised my shamed eyes to hers. Her round, white, rich-lady's face was as concerned for the me of me as a bowl of three-day-old rice pudding might've been. If you left out the raisins.

Now, shoulder to sharp shoulder, that other Willie hastened along beside me toward the Territory of Dakota—opened for settlement with the signing of the Homestead Act by Abe Lincoln in 1862; made reachable by the completion of the Chicago and Northwestern Railroad; as foreign to me as if it were located in the middle of an African desert and populated by camels and people in bedsheets. I leaned forward so that I met my companion nose to nose on the dusty glass.

"I got no hooks anymore on which to hang my life," I told her. "I got lots of parts and pieces and odds and ends, but I got no whole. How will I stick things back together again? Is there a special binder to be used? Does it take a talent I never learned at my orange crate desk behind the boiler at the Tipton County *Tribune* . . . ?"

"Who's that you're talking to, Willie?" TJ bleated fitfully into the folds of my green jacket. "Have Mama and Papa . . ."

"No, TJ," I soothed, a mother before I'd ever been a person of my own. "Mama and Papa have not come back. I just been doing some thinking out loud, asking myself questions that don't have answers."

There was no comment, one way or the other, from that other Willie.

3

"Willie?"

"What?"

"I got to tee-tee."

The train we'd boarded in Tipton had taken us north through Cairo and Evansville and Vincennes to Chicago. Now, having transferred ourselves and our valise to a newer train and having picked up many additional passengers, we were ready to head west for the Territory. And to pinpoint the new location of a toilet. Soon. TJ did not generally sound the alert until he was ready to rain into his shoes.

"Imm'grunts," the big-nosed man across the aisle muttered as we prepared to set out on our quest. "That's what they be, all right. Imm'grunts." He nodded meaningfully toward the rear of the coach.

"Don't gawk," I advised TJ. "It ain't polite. Those folks' origins are not of our immediate concern."

"Sometimes it's Germans, sometimes it's Russians or Swedes. Furriners are taking over the country," Big Nose confided. "This time it's Finns. Trainmaster told me so. Going to the Territory same's the rest of us, to steal a bit of luck. But *Finland.* That's way up there by the Arctic Circle. Sun don't ever shine up there. Them folks are born in the dark and they die in the dark." I knew perfectly well where Finland was. Geography was my next-to-best subject. I knew the sun shone up there at least part of the time.

"And I'm not going to the Territory to steal some luck," I would like to have said. "I'm going there because I got nowhere else to go. It is, strictly speaking, a matter other folks decided. I didn't get to vote yea or nay on it."

TJ reared up on his knees so that he could peek over the back of his seat. I hooked two fingers in his belt and hauled him down again. "Don't gawk," I said.

"But Willie—they are weird! I mean plain, flat-out, no-fooling weird. Look for yourself if you don't believe me."

I was no saint. I looked. The people coming toward us down the aisle were, indeed, like none I'd ever seen in my life. The men wore close-fitting caps made of animal fur, and knee-length coats of the same stuff but with the fur turned inside. All of them, men and women and children, wore high boots of dark horsehair felt that were trimmed brightly with colored braid and embroidery of red and yellow and blue and overhung with tiny golden bells that made a melancholy music each time a foot was raised.

"But their faces," I marveled to TJ, "did you ever in your life see such faces?" Cheekbones high and gleaming, complexions the same burnished color as autumn apples, eyes narrow and somber. I was certain, too, that I could smell those folks: soaked, they were, with the pungent odor of wood fires and faraway pine forests.

The immigrant families descended on TJ and me, led by a man and his wife and a pair of twin girls about TJ's age, whose straw-colored braids stuck out under their kerchiefs. After them came a boy.

As he passed, he stared down at me as curiously as I stared up at him. Maybe it was me who looked weirdest, with my shorn head and hat of faded pink paper roses. His eyes, locked briefly with mine, were the same color I fancied the skies of Finland must be: pale, clear, and cold.

As suddenly as they had appeared they were gone. "To the imm'grunt car," Big Nose told us. "Later, they'll drop off, a family at a time, anywhere there's a spare acre to be settled—Minneapolis, Bismarck, Fargo. Durn furriners!" Then the wistful music of little golden bells was silenced as the wooden door of the coach clanked shut behind them.

But I knew the look I'd gotten from the immigrant boy: I'd seen it in my own bandit eyes whenever they stared back at me from a shard of mirror or a pane of dusty glass. It was the lost and lonesome look of an exile, of one who doesn't belong any place special on the face of the earth. I put my hand to my cheek. It was uncommonly warm.

"You sick, Willie?" TJ chirped. He bent close. His breath dampened my cheek. His eyes, too close to focus, began to cross.

"Back up, TJ. Your eyes are crossing again."

He backed away and brought me into view. "You look funny," he reported. "You going to die on me, too, Willie? Willie, answer me." One pink cheek and he was prepared to plant me. It was a passion that seized hold of him right after Mama and Papa died.

"No, TJ," I said, "I am not going to die. You are stuck with me. Don't borrow trouble. We got enough to last one hundred years as it is."

"Then most certainly we got time to find a toilet," he said, and hopped into the aisle as lively as a flea.

That night, having settled the matter of the toilet's location, and after TJ had fallen asleep and my own knees were tucked under my chin as I tried to do the same, I saw again the eyes of the immigrant boy. I reached into my pocket for a scrap of paper and a pencil. It was too dark to write so I wrote in my head:

His eyes were the same color as I fancied the skies of Finland must be, pale and clear and cold, and he recognized me for what I truly was. Another exile. A person who has lost her place in this world, who belongs no place special on the face of the earth.

I stretched. My knees cracked. I slept.

Twelve hundred miles later, in the hostile hours of a dawn on the sixth of November, our bones arthritic and our flesh smelling sour and unwashed, TJ and I hoisted Papa's valise from the rack over our heads and deposited ourselves in Dakota Territory. The journey had taken twelve nights and thirteen days and had done more than remove us from Tennessee. It had transported us from one life into another.

The train whined off, striking spears of orange flame from the rails as it went. The sky was black and the stars over our heads were hard white prophecies concerning our future. A sharp wind out of the north carried the bright and bitter smell of new snow to our nostrils.

Even in those terrible days right after Mama and Papa died, we had never been so alone. Now TJ snatched for my hand. "Great godamighty, Willie, it's blacker'n a robber's pocket out here. How in the world will Uncle Randall find us in all this dark?"

"He's a reasonable man. He'll wait for the sun to come up."

"But what if he don't know we're here?" TJ persisted. "What if Mr. Rich didn't really send that telegram like he promised he would? What if it got lost? What if . . ."

"You are a worry merchant, TJ."

"What if the Indians capture us?"

"What Indians? I don't see any Indians. No self-respecting Indian would have us."

"Not you, maybe. You got no hair worth mentioning. You ain't worth scalping. But I got hair. Mama said it was pretty as milkweed down." Even in the darkness I was aware that he reached up to protect his precious platinum crown.

"Hush, TJ. Damned if you aren't enough to drive a saint to swearing."

"You're doing it again!" he yelped indignantly and retrieved his paw from mine.

"Doing what?"

"Swearing. Mama and Papa would say it wasn't lady-like. They'd sure hate the way you are carrying on."

"Number one, they shouldn't have called me Willie if they expected me to act like a lady. Number two, I am not carrying on. I am taking charge."

"With you, Willie, it's hard to tell the difference.

And Willie, I been thinking—maybe the fire at the *Tribune* was an accident, just like Mr. Rich said."

"What, pray tell, has that got to do with anything? Of course it was not an accident! I know what I know."

TJ lapsed into silence. As usual, it did not last long. "Willie?"

"What?"

"Will things ever be all right again, Willie?"

I reached for him in the darkness and hauled him close. His head came to rest in the soft triangle just below my breastbone. He was so thin; his heart hammered so hard; he so desperately needed a bath. We got on each other's nerves, which might've happened even if we'd differed less. It seemed not to matter that we were brother and sister, that we were tied together by love and habit that was mostly habit and shy on love; we were just the same trapped by the edges of our own skins and seemed destined to remain strangers to one another.

"How do I know?" I asked back. I tried to put kindness and patience into my voice. "Maybe so, TJ; maybe not. It's too early to tell. But let's at least get in out of this awful bitter wind." I picked up Papa's valise and headed toward the tiny station house that loomed out of the prairie night and bore the dim legend: Red River Junction.

I felt my way along the building to a doorless entry. TJ and I crept inside, but only far enough to get out of the wind. We watched the stars overhead begin to wink out like candles being snuffed. Soon a thin band of green light colored the eastern horizon.

How long had we huddled there before I realized we were not alone? Someone was passing slowly back and forth outside our doorway. Hardly more than the shadow of a someone, a suggestion, a ghost. Then, not a shadow at all, but a flesh and blood stranger stood before us. He peered in at us through the lifting winter gloom, spied us flattened against the wall like a pair of thieves.

It was by no means daylight yet, but I could see all

that I needed to see. I thought weakly of Papa, who was tall and thin and pale, who was a gentleman and a scholar. Uncle Randall was but two years younger and had attended the Boston Conservatory of Music. Without doubt he would look the same. Wouldn't he?

But the man who confronted us was not half a hair taller than I was myself. He did not have a waist like a normal person: everything all up and down was the same size as his stout shoulders, the whole of which was divided into two bandy legs the size of tree trunks. He didn't so much stand there as he was planted there.

Now I had no notion in the world who he was. But sure as the devil has horns I knew who he wasn't. By no means could he be my papa's own dear brother.

"Shoot him, Willie," TJ suggested.

"With what? You seem to forget I am not armed."

"Kick him in the shins. Knock him down. Stomp on him."

Before I could give serious consideration to these suggestions, the stranger posed a question. "Your name Bannerman?" he croaked in a voice seven shades more sinister than any I'd ever heard in my life. His eyes were as small and shiny as the blackberries that grew by Pickle Creek.

"*Who?*" I shrieked.

I gritted my teeth. It was mortifying to think that that hysterical squawk had emanated from me. Then: "Oh. Yes. That is to say, my dear sir, our family name is Bannerman," I explained nervously. "An uncommon one, you may have noticed. Originated back in the olden golden days of England."

The stranger was not impressed, so I clapped an arm firmly around TJ's shoulders. "And this here is Thomas Jefferson Bannerman. Named after the third president of these United States. He's older'n he looks. I mean him, not the president." No one in his right mind would trifle with a boy so filled with honor and history.

But TJ failed to live up to his end of the bargain. His lower jaw had come unhinged and hung level with his coat collar. The smell of fear rose off him like smoke.

"Well." The stranger said it again, as if to confirm the fact in his mind: "Well." He favored us, one at a time, with the thinnest of smiles. He was, I knew, a convict or a horsethief or worse. He also seemed relieved to have found us.

Or was it to have found us *alone?*

4

"Now it was a worry to your uncle, you bet it was," Mr. Convict/Horsethief/or Worse announced, "to know you tads was down here at the junction with no one to meet you. He was terrible sorry not to've been able to come himself. Sent me to fetch you home instead."

TJ rescued his fallen jaw from his coat collar. "Is our uncle sick?" he shrilled. "Dead maybe?" There he went, planting people before he had a chance to shake a hand. "And how come is it you know our uncle?"

The character in the doorway smiled. Only this time the generous and gap-toothed grin he gave us took up his whole face. His blackberry eyes vanished in a network of wrinkles and the empty spaces between his teeth made his smile seem as familiar as a splintered picket fence.

"Sho!" he exclaimed. "Your uncle ain't sick. Not even feeling poorly far's I know. Thing is, see, he's waiting on an old mare about to drop a foal. Didn't want to leave her now her time is due. Old mare that one is, and oughtn't t'be having a foal at all. And me? Well, I do a lick of work for your uncle once in a while and stay to his place when I do. He gives me a corner of the barn to call my own, which suits him and don't pain me none."

As if he considered that that certified him as a reliable escort, the stranger bent down, scooped Papa's valise out of my hand, and trotted toward an old wagon that waited at the end of the station platform.

A tall and melancholy gray mule was hitched to it.
Behind the plain wood seat was a jumble: an empty
barrel, a battered metal washtub, a pile of straw, an assortment of faded blankets that were more hole than
warp and woof.

Now: we had been chauffered out of Tipton County
in the grandest style. In a maroon buggy with painted
yellow wheels, drawn by a tidy red mare named Lady,
driven by the richest man in town.

God forbid Beth Ellen should see me now, I
thought. Beth Ellen, my best friend and a person I
could hardly put up with sometimes. Puppets and pre-
tensions and backyard plays in which she was always
the star. But she happily would never know of my
comedown, on account of I would certainly never tell
her. Vain folk, though, always get their comeuppance
and mine was due: as I hefted TJ onto the seat of the
stranger's wagon, I saw a sight that until that moment
had escaped me.

They must've dropped off in the night, as Big Nose
predicted, and had let their immigrant companions
travel on without them. Now they huddled at the far
end of the platform like rabbits under a briar bush. I
felt the immigrant boy's eyes drill dittoes between my
shoulder blades as we creaked away. *Those eyes are
too old for a boy and too young for a man,* I wrote in
my head. *Like me, he's stuck between being and be-
coming.*

Our escort had no trouble filling the gaps in the conversation and I was relieved to let him run on like a
floody creek. "Guess I ought to introduce myself," he
said. "Call me July. Got a last name, too, but it's hard
to pronounce and a mindbender to spell. And this here
is Sorry." On hearing her name, the old mule flicked
an ear.

"July?" TJ echoed. "Ain't that an awful sissy name
for a growed man?"

July hooted. "Be honest, little man. Would you fool
around with a feller's got a mug like this one?" He
slapped his own cheek sassily with five splayed fingers
that hadn't seen a washbowl in more than a while. He

favored my brother with a fanatic blackberry eye. TJ shriveled, as July intended he should.

"No, sir," he said hastily. "Don't guess I would."

July beamed at us. "Tell you how that name came about. My old ma, she'd had a passel of kids before I showed up and she allowed to Pa after my birthing that she'd run outa names. Call the lad by his birthday month, she told him. And that's what they did." He raised a caterpillar brow. "Coulda been worse, though. Imagine if I'd been born in April. Now even a feller with a face like mine might not've lived that one down."

TJ jerked a thumb in my direction. Watch it," I warned, knowing precisely what he aimed to say, "or I'll lay a bump on your head even a goat couldn't climb."

"Her name's Willie," he piped. " 'Hilly Willie, tall and silly.' That's what Sut Buncher used to holler." I remembered too well. Sut Buncher of the chocolate hair and eyes to match, who had lain in wait behind McDermott's fence and tried to steal two bits from me. For that rashness I left him minus one front tooth.

July peeked over TJ's head and cut me a knowing glance. Why had I imagined he looked wicked? There was something of a shy, if unwashed, gentleman about him. He lifted his hat and massaged a headful of none-too-clean peppersalt curls.

"Ain't her real name, is it?" he asked. "Real name's Willanna, ain't that right?" Willanna. How dear to hear it spoken so far from Tennessee!

"Tell you what, little sister," he said. "You don't take to calling me Julie and I won't call you Willie. Deal?"

"Deal," I said. We kept our bargain, too: he never called me Willie and I never called him Julie. But I never told him I loved him, either, which eventually I came to do.

The road before us, which had started out as not much more substantial than a pair of wagon ruts, now vanished altogether in the thick prairie grass. The sky over our heads, brilliantly blue for November, was swept clean by a few mare's tail clouds. Never before had I seen so much earth and sky crowded together in one place. In Tennessee we had been hugged by the greenness of our smooth hills and the sky was something seen in small patches through the tangled branches of dogwood and butternut and oak.

But more dazzling than the sky of Dakota Territory was its grass. As far as we could see, it stretched in every direction, a dense and waist-high stand of copper-colored grass. It surrounded us on every side like a burnished ocean, undulating and flowing with an undersea life of its own.

Hereabouts they call it prairie hay," July told us. Harvest it just like the domestic kind, only it's even better feed for livestock." He squinted across that red sea and seemed to have something on his mind.

"You two have come to make a new home in a contrary land," he said. "Can test human beings like nothing in this world. Folks believe they can come to the Territory to make a fortune. Land is cheap, they think, and it'll all be duck soup. And some do make it big. But there's a dozen more that don't. They're the ones go crazy or go back where they came from in the first place."

There was something I had to know. Quick.

"My . . . our uncle, Mr. Bannerman. Is he one of them who made it big?"

July did not look at me. "Your uncle?" He pulled on the end of his nose. "Little sister, let me put it to you this way. All your uncle needs is a fast track and a little bit of luck. He might find it easier if . . ."

He would have pursued the matter further, but at that moment there came to our ears a racket that pulsed right out of the heart of the rising sun. I craned my neck over my shoulder and shielded my eyes.

A solitary rider was coming hard at us through the shifting sea of red prairie hay. Uncle Randall, no doubt, with good news about the foal he'd helped to get born. In another moment, however, I could plainly see the rider was not a man. It was a fierce and hell-

for-leather female of uncertain age and questionable
disposition who stripped a battered black hat from her
head and waved it wildly in the chilly autumn air.

She hallooed to us in a clear, commanding voice.
Her hair, just the same copper color as the prairie hay,
tumbled over her shoulders. A bright blue and yellow
scarf was knotted around her neck, the ends of which
floated out behind her like the wings of an enormous
butterfly.

"Who is that?" I demanded. But my startled heart
already knew. Hadn't Mr. Rich tried to warn us? *A
most unusual woman. . . .*

July confirmed my worst suspicions. "Little sister,
that is a lady who plans to be a legend in her own
time—if she's got a word to say about it, that is. And
she usually does."

Let me admit, here and now, there were certain matters I never discussed with TJ. He was only six and a
sissy to boot. I did not confess, for instance, that during each of those twelve hundred miles from Tennessee
a dread had plagued me. It was brewed up out of all
the fictions and fables I'd ever heard about cruel kin-
folk, wicked stepmothers, and assorted malicious souls
whose main occupation in life it was to torment poor,
unfortunate orphans.

*I know all I need to know about how orphans get
beaten up and eaten up and locked away in damp,
dark places,* I thought every night as we headed west.
In no way do I need to try the experience on for size.

Now, ready or not, I was about to confront the
wicked lady of our future. TJ, lucky little duck, was
the sort of child poets write about, with his fanciful
hair and his violet eyes, and was still young enough to
be molded to suit other folks' fond desires. I was
putty-eyed and plain and too far gone over the hill to
be changed by the most well-meaning soul.

The woman July had called Belle Bannerman hauled
up beside our wagon. She reined her pony in so hard
he rose skyward like an arrow, eyes ringed with white
as his hooves clawed the empty sky. He came down

with a thump on all fours and I found myself staring smack into a narrow, white female face level with my own.

It surely was not like any of the faces in my nightmares. Not old or wrinkled or warty at all. Its cheeks were dusted brightly with nutmeg freckles, its nose sassy and sharp, its chin dimpled, and it was all lighted up by two wild, clear eyes the color of fresh mint jelly. I reached aside to scoop TJ into my arms. He would be more startled even than me.

I was too late. TJ's open mouth and round eyes were shaped into three perfect *O*'s of love and amazement. He had been bewitched.

"Aunt Belle?" he whispered, as though she was a haunt he would frighten away. "You that lady Mr. Rich said was fixing to be our Aunt Belle?"

Lord, Lord. It was all the encouragement that hide-and-bone female needed. She reached across the empty space that separated her from my brother, plucked him neatly off the wagon bench with a pair of long, strong arms, and, enchanted herself, smiled into his face.

"Does a dog have fleas?" she cried. "I am indeed Belle Bannerman! The one and only! Even the Territory of Dakota ain't big enough to hold more'n one of my kind. But you!" She surveyed him happily. "Ain't you a *picture?* Just like I told Mr. B. you'd be!" She planted a noisy kiss right in the middle of TJ's forehead and then, over the top of his head, skewered me on the end of a shrewd, jellymint stare.

With her sharp nose and narrow green eyes she looked altogether like a fierce and clever fox. But when she smiled, as she did at that very moment, such uncommon sweetness filled her face that it pinched my heart.

"You must be Willie." Her puzzlement was plain. "Willie." She said my name again, as if the fact were in some dispute.

Then, while she hugged TJ snugly to her with one hand, she reached up with the other to touch my shorn head. She did not ask, then or ever, "What happened?"

Never said to me, "Stars and garters, what sort of madness made you mutilate yourself in such a way?" She never had to. Concerning such frailties of the human spirit, Belle Bannerman was an expert.

5

Belle was not out on the prairie on such a brisk morning merely to act as a one-woman committee to welcome me and TJ to the Territory. She turned, crisp and full of business, to July.

"Mr. B.'s waiting on you, July," she said. "Foal hadn't been born by the time I left and it looked to me like we might lose Fanny, too. Here—you take my pony and hasten back to help. I'll get the children home safe and sound."

So saying, she plunked TJ back on the wagon bench and threw down her pony's reins. As soon as July got down from his seat she leaped up beside me to take his place.

"Don't dither a minute," she advised, "and just hope and pray you ain't already too late." July obediently mounted up, put her black pony into a smart trot, and soon disappeared in the head-high stand of prairie hay.

TJ and I tried our best not to stare bug-eyed at the lady called Belle Bannerman, but it was a losing game. In no way did Mr. Rich's warning prepare us for the likes of her. One minute her profile might be sharp as a knife blade against the sky, the next minute we would find ourselves impaled on the end of a ferocious green glance.

"Glad you came to the Territory?" she demanded to know.

"Oh, yes, ma'am," I answered quickly for both of us. It seemed to be what she wanted to hear. But how could I know yet if we were glad or not?

"In the beginning, *I* was scared," she confessed sassily. "Scared of all the space. The wind. The weather. You ain't lived through nothing till you've lived through a Dakota winter!" Her eyes narrowed. "But a fortune can be made on the prairie, and that's what me and Mr. B aim to do. Don't aim to be all hat and no cattle forever, let me tell you! Them bonanza farmers from back East—bankers and brokers who pool their money and buy up acres by the thousands—well, they ain't the only ones can make it big! Someday we'll build a house that'll put those bonanza fellers to shame—all porches and pillars and stained glass in the front door!"

Her zest was infectious and I did not doubt her for a second. But when she cried out a moment later and directed our eyes to the west, I began to wonder.

"There it is—there's House Place! The beginning of the great Bannerman empire!"

She pointed energetically with her whole arm. I squinted and shaded my eyes. I couldn't see a blamed thing. Only a wide, grassy prairie that was slightly rolling in contour, without a tree or a shrub or a bush as far as I could see. Then I *did* see.

Where the land began to slope gently toward a shallow creek bed, there emerged a low, disheveled dwelling fashioned higgledy-piggledy out of tar paper, sod, logs, and galvanized tin. It crouched against the slope of earth like a beast about to spring from its lair. Weeds and frost-blackened sunflowers drooped from its dirt-covered roof. Sorry, knowing she was almost home, began to hurry.

"It ain't like you promised me it'd be, Willie," TJ complained loudly in my ear.

"What's that you say, sweetie?" Belle asked.

"He just wondered how soon we'd be there," I said. TJ was right, of course: there was no fine house set in the middle of a green acre of lawn. No flowers as big as my head. No pony cart painted green, no forest of chinaberry trees.

Instead, the front door of House Place looked out upon a small sod barn and the ground between the two was worn as hard and bare as city pavement. There wasn't a thing growing in that space except a single discouraged clump of knotweed.

"House Place!" Belle exulted, not seeing what we saw. "Your home for as long as you want it to be!" I cranked up the corners of my mouth in a smile.

"Yes, ma'am. It was mighty gracious of you to take us in, too."

We hadn't managed to climb down from the wagon before July hustled himself outside the barn. "Better come quick, Miss Belle. Fetch some rags, too," he said. "I guess it's too late for Fanny, but maybe we can still save the foal."

Belle jumped down and ran into the house, skirt flapping around her legs, and reappeared a minute later with an armful of coarse rags. "You children wait inside the house," she hollered over her shoulder. "You probably ought not be witness to this." She vanished into the barn.

"Ought not be witness to what, Willie?" TJ wondered.

"That foal trying to get itself born," I said, peeved. Ought not to witness a birth, for Lord's sake, when we'd already witnessed a pair of murders? Such logic did not make a pea particle of sense to me. I jumped down and held my arms up for TJ.

"C'mon, Bubba," I said through clenched teeth. "Let's go and see if there isn't something we can do to help."

The inside of the barn was saved from inky darkness only by the dim light of a single smoky kerosene lantern that hung from a wooden peg pounded into the dirt wall. A trio of speckled chickens roosted on the top of a stall that held a small brown cow. The mare we'd heard called Fanny, an enormous dark and groaning creature, lay prone in the straw with all four legs braced stiffly from her body. Both July and the man who must be Uncle Randall but whose face we could not see were bent over her in consternation.

"And it beats me how this old gal got with foal in the first place," July was saying. "Been barren as long

as anyone can remember and sold cheap to you for
that very reason. Ain't nature's way, neither, to drop a
foal as winter's chill is coming on."

Belle leaned over the men and the mare, her hands
propped on her knees, her furled butterfly wings folded
on her shoulders. The mare filled the barn with rusty,
worn-out sighs. Belle shook her head. "Seems like that
foal just doesn't want to get itself born, doesn't it?"

My uncle, whose face remained a mystery, spoke up.
"We got to do something, July. Fanny can't last much
longer. She's too weak to give one more push. She'll go
and take the foal with her if we don't figure out something. . . ." That voice! It was Papa's selfsame voice,
filled with puzzlement and determination. Three
months rolled away as though they'd never been.

July straightened himself and rolled up his sleeves.
"You set right there, Mr. B., and hang onto her head.
Talk easy to her. Comfort her as best you're able. I'll
do what's necessary."

The old brown mare moaned feebly and bore down
one last time on the reluctant foal in her belly. I wondered if that unseen creature (was it brown, like its
mother? roan? sorrel?) knew what a winter in Dakota
Territory was like and therefore refused to oblige the
world by its appearance.

July knelt at the mare's haunches while Belle held
the lantern close. He reached deep into the mare's di-
lated birth canal in an effort to tempt the foal from the
warm, dark haven of its mother's body. He seized hold
of the foal's tiny black forehooves and pulled gently.
The old mare's groans began to fade.

July pulled again. Gentle, insistent, determined.
Again, nothing happened. Once more he tugged, knees
braced wide apart. Then, so sudden and swift that it
appeared to involve no effort or pain at all, the tiny
creature slid from the shelter of its dam's body and out
onto the clean, dry straw that was spread to receive it.
It lay there, wet and silent and shining, in the dim
circle of light cast by the kerosene lantern.

"It's a filly, sure enough," July told us. "Who
knows, might be as good a worker as her old ma has

been." He stripped the filmy birth sac from the foal's tiny muzzle while Belle put the lamp back on its peg and snatched up some of the rags she'd carried from the house. She began to try to rub some life into the filly's motionless limbs.

"Sure looks poorly to me," she said. "Poor winter babe—I think the hard birth might've been too much for her."

The mare, too weak to get to her feet, called urgently to the foal she could not see. There was no answer from the damp bundle that Belle labored over. The mare called again. Again. Each time there was a wilder note of grief in her cry. But suddenly, in a crazy, mixed-up flurry of straw and rags and four long legs that went in every direction at once, the foal stood up.

We stared.

The barn was silent save for the murmurings of the speckled hens. None of us could think of the proper thing to say. In the amber circle of light thrown by the lantern, that newborn filly gleamed as pale and silvery as a phantom. She was a little never-was right out of some tale told in the Tennessee pinewoods when the moon was full.

She snorted daintily and I flinched. Her nostrils flared to show tender scarlet linings. Her tail, no more than a saucy silver brush, whisked impudently to and fro. She inspected me with two large dark eyes as shy and astonished as a pair of wet morning glories.

"Now ain't she prettier'n a pig in a petunia patch!" July exclaimed.

"It's snowbirds she puts me in mind of," Belle said. "When I was a girl they used to come down every year from the north. Floated in like mist off the sea. Settled in fields and on fences and sometimes right on a body's doorstep. My pa said back home in Ireland folks believed such birds could change a man's fortune."

For some reason I could not tack a name to, my heart had gotten a trifle too large for my brisket. Wedged under a rib, it was, making it tolerably hard to breath. I rammed my fist deep into the pocket of my thin, green Tennessee jacket and encountered there a sharp object. Two days after the blaze at the Tipton County *Tribune,* when the ashes were still warm from the fire, I had retrieved from them a piece of twisted typeset. My fingers traced letters that had been melted together into hieroglyphics as mysterious as those on an Egyptian pharaoh's tomb.

The blood and bones and brains of William and Anna Bannerman are forged into this piece of lead, that other Willie reminded me. *It is your only legacy from two people who made a name for you and who believed to their death in dreaming and telling.*

But hadn't I been inventing people and places and events a long time back? Such dealings and doings as existed only inside my own head? Figments, Mama had called them. Maybe I was doing it again. I looked over my shoulder at the filly. She regarded me with wet, black surprised eyes.

"The Snowbird," I heard someone say. It must have been Belle. "The Snowbird . . . now don't it seem like it was meant to be her name? With none of us knowing for sure where she came from or where she's bound? The Snowbird. How could we ever call her anything else?" It was my own voice, rusty and ragged as a stranger's in my ears.

My uncle lifted his eyes to the light. That face was the same as Papa's, only younger. Shadows like blue bruises under the eyes. High cheekbones. A forehead wide and white with worry written all across it. And starting that night, since it was the only way I ever heard him called, he became Mr. B. to me.

"Maybe Willie's right," he said. "The Snowbird— who's come to Dakota Territory to change our fortunes." It was plain from the way he said the words that he wanted to believe them even more than I did.

6

I came awake with a pounding heart. I lay stiff as a corpse in my coffin of warm quilts. TJ's haunch rested companionably against my own. I strained my eyes hard into the blackness over my head. From what seemed like a great distance I could hear someone singing in a high, sweet voice that was relentlessly off key:

> I know where I'm going and I know who's going with me,
> I know who I love but the devil knows who I'll marry;
> I'll wear stockings of silk and shoes of fine green leather,
> But I would leave them all for my handsome, winsome
> Johnnie....

I rolled over to the trapdoor opening where a narrow wooden ladder descended from the attic into the kitchen below. I found myself staring down on a turban of outrageous red braids. My uncle's name was Randall. *Who was handsome, winsome Johnnie . . . ?*

She must have felt the weight of my eyes on the top of her head, for she turned to look up at me with a sly fox grin. Her eyes were more green and glazed than they had seemed yesterday at our first meeting.

"Ready to rise and shine, luv?" she asked.

Luv. I peered down at her as suspicious as a Christmas goose. Mama and Papa, who had loved me in their fashion, never spoke to me so sassily.

"Wake up the lad while you're at it," Belle went on, "and we three will set ourselves down for some victuals. July and Mr. B. have already hied themselves to the barn to see after that filly."

Ah. So I had dreamed none of it. Last night, in blood and groans and rusty sighs, welcomed into this world by a circle of amber light and the scrutiny of five pairs of anxious eyes, a silver horse had been born. I stretched a leg back into the darkness of the attic cave and stabbed TJ with my big toe.

"Get up, Bubba," I commanded.

He stirred and cried out, "I smell something good, Willie! Has Mama . . ."

"No, TJ. Mama ain't come back. We're at House Place now and Belle's got our breakfast cooking."

I pulled my skirt on, yanked my warm wool socks up over my knees, jerked a sweater over my head. I considered the room I'd slept in at Mr. Rich's. Its walls had been baby blue, the woodwork was painted white, the curtains were crisp organdy dotted with rows of tiny cotton puffs. A chinaberry tree grew right outside the window; from it birds sang me awake every morning of the three months I slept there. It also was the first and final time I had a room of my own.

"It isn't fit, you know, a girl your size should be sleeping with a brother," Mrs. Rich had whispered to me. Her eyes were accusing. Was she afraid I would roll over in the night and crush the life out of him? Might smother him like folks claim a cat will suffocate a brand-new baby? TJ wasn't *that* small. Or was that her point?

The room in which I presently found myself was not a room at all. It was simply a small, cramped loft over the kitchen, warmed only by the heat radiating from the chimney that came up and passed through a lop-sided hole cut in the floor. It did not matter, of course. I would be roosting in this loft but a short while. Other things were bound to happen. I would grow up, among others. Move away. Take TJ with me. I was descended from the likes of James Robertson and Pauline Cushman. I was accountable.

When TJ was assembled, we clambered down the ladder into the kitchen. Thick chunks of rosy ham were frying in a pan on the stove. Coffee, steaming and fragrant, bubbled in a foot-high pot of robin's egg blue. Griddlecakes, fringed at their edges with brown lace, were stacked on a cracked white plate in the warming oven.

"Come, stand here beside my Herschvogel and warm yourselves," Bell invited. *Herschvogel?* "Don't you remember the stove in the fairy story?" she asked, seeing my look. Of course I remembered. Only I hadn't expected to meet the Grimm brothers' stove in the middle of Dakota Territory.

Belle flew about the room, thin as a whip, her bared arms lean and lightly freckled, to set plates and mugs for TJ and me. "Now I grant to you that House Place may not seem very special," she said, reading my mind, "especially since you have so recently come from Mr. Rich's." Then, as an aside, she added, "I never quite liked Mr. Rich. His eyes reminded me of raisins. Tiny. Pinched." She dumped Mr. Rich and galloped on with her original topic. "Later I'll show you the place where we'll build a real house. Later, when we have lots of money. Then we'll have enough space to have our own circus if we take a notion!"

Madam, it sounds like a capital idea, I thought. For how can you call one square room a house? On its inside, House Place had no walls or rooms. Instead, each of its four corners fulfilled some purpose: under a small window with cloudy panes a packing crate had been converted into a table. Chairs without backs or arms had been fashioned from nail kegs. In another corner stood a brass bed as big as a boat in which Belle and Mr. B. slept. Beside it was a dresser with a cracked yellow mirror and at its foot was a trunk with a brass lock as big as my fist. In the third corner was a washstand, bucket, and metal dipper. Two nails with a length of string stretched between made a towel rack. In the fourth corner was a door, reinforced with a Z brace. The entire dwelling was no more than sixteen feet square.

Poor Willie! a voice commiserated sweetly in my ear. *I never thought it'd come to this!* Beth Ellen again. Her talented tongue had always been able to make my life narrower than it had to be. Why had I never stole back the power I gave her to shrink everything I thought or saw or did?

Belle studied me while I studied the house. "You got wise eyes, my girl," she said. Widow Wilson had called them old. Well. Truly, I did not feel wise or old either one. *Dear Beth Ellen: I am enjoying my new life in Dakota Territory. It is everything I figured it would be. You'll have to come and see me sometime.* (Knowing she never would and I was safe.) *P.S. I have my own horse. A filly, all white, except for black points on her ears. Prettier than anything I ever saw in Tennessee.*

Belle heaped food onto our plates. "Grab a root and growl," she called.

"Ma'am?" TJ inquired, hands held white-knuckled behind his back.

"Means come and eat," Belle told him. Her voice was filled with smiles. "Like, what did one bear say to the other bear? Grab a root and growl."

"Yes, ma'am!" TJ agreed, loving her with round violet eyes as he forked ham into his mouth. *Be careful, TJ,* I wanted to warn. *Don't love her too much. Don't you know by now what love can do to you?*

Mama and Papa, not to mention the Riches, had never set out coffee for TJ and me. Now Belle filled a pair of mugs to the brim for us, poured in thick, yellow cream, added sugar, and stirred it all around. We washed down our griddlecakes and potatoes and ham with that hot and syrupy drink. Even now, after so much time has gone by, to fetch up the memory of our first meal at House Place, to turn it over and over in my palm like a moss agate collected from the Red River, is enough to provoke me to happiness.

As soon as we had finished Belle tossed off her apron. "Can't wait to lay these green peepers on that Snowbird," she said. "It's an omen, don't you think?

Her coming to us on the very same day you two show up? A good omen. I believe in such things, you know: omens and happy endings and pots of gold at the end of rainbows."

We three entered the barn as gingerly as house-breakers. The speckled hens and their rooster scratched in the straw and murmured to one another in tones people use in church. Steam rose off the back of the brown cow tied in the corner. The eyes of July's mule and Belle's black pony were as many-faceted as jewels. And the old mare was on her feet, weak and weaving, but able to give suck to her foal.

And I would be a liar if I did not confess right now that there was something peculiar about that foal. In the dim light of the barn, surrounded by our soft breathing and the conversation of the speckled chickens, she seemed to glow as though lit by a lamp from within.

"Magic," Belle whispered. "Just plain, old Irish magic. That's what she's all about."

"I reckon we got a hold of something special this time, Belle," Mr. B. said. "Something that was due us." Although there were four of us to whom he might have spoken, it was always Belle who received his remarks. Then he smiled Papa's young-old smile and winked at her. "And I've heard it's good luck to meet a red-haired lady riding a white horse."

Belle clapped her thigh with glee. "Now wouldn't I look grand! I'd be something no one in the whole township would ever forget!" She whirled on me, eyes extravagant in her pale face. "But this ain't really my horse. Willie named her; Willie should have her. I hereby bequeath her to Willie." *Did you hear that, Beth Ellen? It wasn't a lie. I do have my own horse. Silver. Lit by a lamp from within.*

July had more practical interests on his mind, such as the genesis of the Snowbird. "When the Browns owned her mama and even later when the Smalleys took her—always barren. Not only that, a white foal ain't much of a commonplace. Maybe this filly's papa was that pacing white mustang Josiah Gregg, the newspaper feller, wrote about. Most likely, though, ain't none of us ever going to know for sure the origins of the stud that planted a seed in Fanny's belly."

I knew.

Of course I did. I'd already written the story sixteen times in my head. "Bet it was a runaway Sioux stallion," I said. "Silver he was, descended no doubt from a great-grandsire that'd been fetched to this continent from Andalusia. Carried across the ocean in the gloomy hold of some leaky Spanish galleon. Might've been ridden right up that sandy beach in Florida by Ponce de León himself. Got loose later when everyone took off on that crazy goose hunt through the Everglades looking for the Fountain of Youth. Sure, that's probably the way it was. Later he sired sons and daughters by Sioux and Kiowa and Arapaho mares who had sons and daughters of their own, some carrying the silver seeds of their great-grandfather. What we got here right now is a throwback to that first Spanish stallion, all silver and moondust and hope."

My yarn left everyone speechless. "Willie," Belle sighed at last, "I must say you got quite an imagination."

"She got figments, too," TJ said.

"They anything like lice?" July wondered.

"Nope. Figments are inside her head."

"Sholey, that makes 'em different all right. Lice is usually on the outside."

"Figments are good to have," TJ declared helpfully. "Willie's writing a book, see, and you got to have figments for that." After the fire I had tried my best to teach that boy to keep his own counsel. It had been, truth to tell, like fitting socks on a rooster.

"A book?" Mr. B. echoed. He pondered me as though he'd never clapped two eyes on me before.

The conversation had definitely gone too far down the wrong road, so I dropped to my knees in the straw and called out to the filly. "Here, girl. Come here, Bird. Come to Willie. Atta girl. Ain't no one here ever going to hurt you." How could I know I would be the only one to ever break that pledge?

The Snowbird studied me serenely. No shadow of antic wildness lighted her morning glory eyes. She moved toward me and stopped only when her slim silver face was inches from my own. Her warm, sweet milkbreath brushed my cheek, soft as one of TJ's prayers.

"Is she going to stay this way?" I whispered. "So quiet and unafraid?"

"Most horses ain't afraid of human beings in the first few hours after their birth," July said. "She might learn fear after a spell or might never learn it at all. I reckon horses ain't no different than people in that respect. Some folks are born mild and tame, some come into this world as scrappers and fighters. Why, I know one or two who'll argue life to a draw and ask for a rematch!"

I looked up in time to see Belle toss him a glance hot enough to hatch an egg. Her chin was up and her mouth was a narrow, unlovely line. "I'm a fighter and a scrapper," that green glare declared, "and I make no apologies for it."

I placed a kiss on the tip of the filly's small, damp muzzle. *What about me?* I asked her silently. *Am I a fighter or a weak sister? Belonger or still a misfit, up my own tree, alone? Or just some no-hair sort of person even the Sioux wouldn't trifle with?* Something in me persisted in the asking of questions that had no answers. It was a hard habit to break.

Christmas arrived six weeks later and TJ and I each received a fragrant orange and an almond for good luck. Belle dispatched one of the speckled hens and stuffed it with cornbread and chopped giblets and a sprig of wild sage plucked by July from the snowy roof of House Place. Mr. B. presented Belle with a tiny blue enamel lapel watch he said he'd purchased many months before when his funds were more numerous. The hands beneath its raised crystal orb were gold and the numbers, likewise of gold, were garlanded with pink rosebuds and entwined by tiny green leaves.

"So you will never forget what time it is," Mr. B. told her with a young-old smile. Belle studied him from behind the screen of her fierce green eyes. I hoped that she loved him, too.

7

That year, spring came like a blessing to the prairie. What one day was flat and fierce and inhospitable to man and beast alike became beautiful with windflowers, chicory, blazing stars, and fleabane. Even the earth between House Place and the barn, hard as a piece of sheet iron throughout the long winter, blossomed with doorgrass, and House Place's sod roof sprouted a fresh halo of black-eyed daisies.

And in that time, the spring of 1884, the Snowbird became a girlchild, being six months old, or equal to more than three years of age if she'd been a human creature.

"Won't be long, now the weather's decent, that we ought to be thinking of halter-breaking that filly," Mr. B. allowed one evening at supper. "July can do it, of course. July's forgotten more about horseflesh than the rest of us'll ever know." He mopped up the gravy on his plate with the flattened edge of a biscuit. July, who sat across the table, regarded the compliment as lightly as he did the black half-moons beneath his fingernails.

"On the other hand, Willie," Mr. B. mused, "would you care to take on the job? That is, if you don't have anything else planned?"

What plans, pray tell, was I going to have, fourteen years of age and no place special to go? Nevertheless, I sidled up to his left-handed offer with an indifference calculated to save my pride just in case he was joshing.

"Well, yes," I allowed, careful to register no particular enthusiasm for the job. "I suppose I might manage to do it, sir."

"You don't have to call me sir, Willie." He looked at me as he often did, surprised to find me sitting there at his own supper table. "I'm your papa's brother. Your uncle. It isn't necessary for you to call me sir."

"I always called Papa sir, sir."

"You did?" He was amazed. "But why?"

"Papa set great store on acting civilized, sir. Said it saved the day when tempers got hot." It was another of those remarks Papa made that I never truly understood.

Mr. B. shook his head. His lips were fixed in the vulnerable smile that was so familiar to me, and there was in his eyes a tearful look that appeared whenever we chanced to talk of my father.

"There was so much I didn't know about William," he said. "We grew rather apart, you see, after . . ."

"After you married me," Belle finished for him. It seemed to be a conversation they'd had before.

"You really aim to let ol' Willie halter-break that filly?" TJ wanted to know, not minding that his conversation went at right angles with what had just been said.

"Certainly, if she'd like to so do," Mr. B. answered, not looking up again.

"I do. I do." I said it quickly before he changed his mind. "That is, if July will show me what to do and when to do it."

The next morning when I walked across the yard to the barn, the Snowbird and Fanny were taking the early sun on their backs. When the Bird spied me coming, she began to make spirited turns around and around the corral, her featherduster tail lifted high and shimmering in the air, head raised, neck arched. She was like some people I'd known, female people, who knew how beautiful they were. Belle. Beth Ellen. I'd envied Beth Ellen until it felt like a canker sore. To know I was ten times smarter hadn't helped a pea particle.

July waited for me at the corral gate, a strange-looking contraption dangling from one grimy hand.

"What's that?" I asked. It didn't look like much of anything at all to me, just a jing-jangle of ropes and straps, each hooked to the other by rusty rings rescued off ancient harnesses or saddle gear.

"This here is a halter," he informed me.

"Halter, my handspring," I tossed back. Didn't I remember the one Mr. Rich used for his tidy red mare? A veritable sculpturing of tooled leather with smart brass doodads? What I was looking at now was a gypsy contrivance invented out of cast-off junk that'd lain idle for Lord knows how long in the corner of the barn or maybe in the back of July's own wagon.

"Get your snoot down outta the air," he advised me. "Ain't no sense in Mr. B. investing good money in a foal halter when I can throw one together quick as I can skin a rabbit. The Snowbird's gonna outgrow it almost before we get her all halter-broke anyhow." He fastened me with a no-nonsense, Pickle-Creek-blackberry eye. "Now—you ready to commence with this job?"

"Won't know for sure until I try, will I?" I snapped. I was waspish when there was no need to be. "You just give me a few pointers and I'll do the best I can. I don't know all that much about horses; Papa didn't have one of his own, see, until after he began to investigate the scandal. Just went out and rented a horse off someone else. Said there wasn't any sense to feeding one every day whether he rode it or not."

"Sounds like a man after my own heart," July said. Then, after a moment of silence, came the question I knew would follow. "Scandal, you say? Now what sort of scandal would that be, sis?"

"The one that put him in an early grave and my mother right behind him," I muttered in a way that discouraged further discussion of the subject. How could I explain it to him when mostly I still didn't understand it myself? Railroads and kickbacks and labor contracts that weren't paid for and all that collusion. (Was a collusion like a collision? Maybe so. Papa and

Mama had sure been wiped out by it.) All those things Mama and Papa talked about late at night when they were sure I was asleep but wasn't. It was a puzzle to me still, even though I had taken pains to convince Mr. Rich I knew things I didn't know at all.

July was gentleman enough to let my testiness pass. He handed the halter to me. "Never knew why folks talk about breaking a horse," he said, changing the subject easy as he'd swat a fly. "I mean, would you go out and buy yourself a set of broken dishes? You want a busted chair to sit on, maybe? A broken bed to sleep in? Not unless you got green cheese between your ears you don't. Break a horse? Naw. Train a horse? Takes longer, but you got something to depend on when you do." I imagined it was the longest speech he'd ever made.

We walked together toward the corral gate where the filly and Fanny waited for us. July crossed his arms over the top rung and I did the same. I had aged several years already.

"Now the whole idea is to get the filly used to having something on her head," July said. "We also got to accustom her to being led on a rope and being separated from her ma's side. Sounds easy—and might turn out that way, too. Only recollect the Snowbird's been free as a bee since that day we pulled her into this world. You ready to commence, sis?"

"Ready as I'm ever going to be." My palms were greasy.

July showed me how to hold the halter and how to pass it over her head. "Walk up to her nice and easy, just like you was fixing to give her a brushing. Let her see what you got in your hand. Don't try to trick her. Let her smell of it; let her know what it is."

That part surely would not be hard, for the Snowbird dearly loved to have her face and her head rubbed and tickled. She held her head out, in fact, begging to be fondled. I straightened her silvery forelock and rubbed her poll, which made her close her eyes in dreaming.

"Now's the time to slide the halter onto her head," July coached from his place at the gate.

While the Snowbird was relishing the loving I gave her, I eased the gypsy rig onto her head. She barely blinked. I fastened the buckle at her cheek. She gave her head a mild shake. *Such an aggravation,* she seemed to say. When that did not rid her of the peskiness of the halter, she shook harder and reached out in protest to scratch her cheek against my arm.

"I don't think she's going to like this," I said.

"That don't matter. She'll get used to it in time."

But instead of holding her head up proud and sassy as was her custom, the Snowbird let it dangle out on the end of her neck as though she wasn't sure what to do with it anymore. "Now fasten the lead rope to the halter," July instructed. "Let her feel the weight of it for a minute. Stand directly in front of her so's not to twist her neck in case she rears back. Then walk her around the corral."

I did precisely as he directed. I pulled gently on the halter rope. Just as gently, the Snowbird pulled back. I obliged by tugging a wee bit more deliberately. She resisted even more firmly. I fastened my heels into the dirt and urged her forward with my whole body. Nothing, of course, happened.

July whooped softly and whacked his hat against his knee. "She ain't going to fight with you; it ain't her style. But she sure ain't going to give you no cooperation neither!" He did not seem disturbed. "Leave her alone now. Unclip the rope but leave the halter on her. Maybe she needs to think about it a spell. We'll come back tonight after chores are done; maybe she'll be in a better frame of mind."

The sky was lavender and barn swallows shot through it like spent arrows before I got the supper dishes put away. It pleased me mightily to see House Place blessed with barn swallows. Meant we'd never be struck by lightning, if what the hillfolk of Tipton County said was true.

As soon as I stepped into the yard I could hear the tinkle of buckles and rings on the gypsy halter. The

Snowbird stood in the center of the corral, head lowered, still peeved.

Why in the world are you doing me like this? her vexed glance asked me.

"You're a horse and I'm an orphan and we both got our own little bucket o' woes, that's why," I told her. "You think I got it so easy? Living in a land that don't have a single chinaberry tree to its name? Least *you* can do is learn to wear a halter!"

She had her own ideas about that philosophy. With a snort, the Snowbird lifted her hind heels in the air and struck willfully at the sky. Then off she went, nipping and tucking around the corral.

"She don't think much of your religion," July called out to me from his corner of the barn.

"Let's take the blamed thing off her," I said. "She won't even look at me anymore."

"By morning she might have a different perspective," he said.

Belle, who had come out of the house behind me, spoke up at my elbow. "Seems a shame, don't it?" she mused. "Some of the Lord's creatures ought never be anything but wild."

Together we studied the Snowbird—me in a snit of disappointment, Belle viewing a landscape I could not see. I cut a glance her way. Her white profile was sharp as an ax blade against the darkening sky. Those green eyes, seen cross-section by me, were clear and tranquil as the eyes of the china doll I'd admired one Christmas in a store window in Memphis when I was seven. Later Mama and Papa bought it for me to make up for TJ. It hadn't helped much.

"If you love a thing, you set it free," Belle said. "If it comes back to you, it's yours. If it doesn't, it was never meant to be."

The night was warm for May, but I shivered. I knew she wasn't speaking to me. Or about the Snowbird. I shut my ears tight. I did not want to think about what she meant.

8

"A book," Mr. B. speculated to me. I cringed. TJ's revelation of my bookwriting ambitions had taken place six months before. But Mr. B. had not forgotten, as I'd hoped he would. Talked about in the bright light of a spring afternoon, those notions seemed as mangy as a barn cat.

"Yessir," TJ said, meddling again. It was his only talent. "Willie's set on making a memorial. To Mama and Papa. Only I won't even know what it says because I can't read. Willie claims she's gonna be famous someday, like that ol' Lou-ezza Who-ezza."

"Lou *Who?*" Mr. B. echoed.

"Louisa May Alcott," I explained. I felt obliged, too, to defend myself. "Papa said dreams don't have to die," I said. "Not as long as there's a person left to do the dreaming, and someone left to do the telling."

Mr. B.'s pale forehead became mottled with pink and his eyes reddened. "There was a great deal, I guess, that I didn't know about William. That I should have known."

"Dreaming and telling?" Belle sniffed. "Doesn't sound like it ever put a penny in anybody's pocket. Matter of fact, it sent your brother to an early grave and made a pair of orphans out of his children."

"Mr. Rich said Papa was a gentleman. A scholar, too," TJ piped. "I know what a gentleman is. A man like Mr. Rich, who wears nice clothes and smells fine. Only what's a scholar?"

Mr. B. gave TJ's arm an affectionate squeeze. I regretted that I was too old and too starchy to receive such a caress.

"A scholar? Why, I guess that's a man who loves things of the mind. A man who's looking for what cannot be seen with the eye. A searcher and a seeker: yes, that is what your papa was. A searcher and a seeker."

"Might as well look for the sun at midnight as search after some things," Belle observed.

Mr. B. apologized for her with a smile. "I know, Belle. I know," he soothed. "But if Willie wants to write a book and if TJ here wants to read it, why, then, we are going to have to send them to school."

"Neither one of them has got the proper clothes for school," she objected. "Besides, the school term is over for the year. They'll have to wait until next fall."

Mr. B. nodded. "Nevertheless, I intend to go to Red River tomorrow to get garden seeds and such like. Willie can go with me and we will make the necessary arrangements."

"Takes money to send them to school," Belle warned. "Books and clothes and lunch buckets ain't given away for nothing." It was one of the many times I would hear discussed between Belle and Mr. B. the matter of money. How to make it. When to keep it. Where to spend it. Money was king and queen and jack of diamonds at House Place.

"The children have a bit of inheritance from their father," Mr. B. said. It was the first I'd heard of such a thing. "Mr. Rich sent it to me before they got here."

"You never mentioned a word of it to me," Belle marveled.

"The money wasn't ours, Belle." Whether she forgave Mr. B. or not, I do not know, for with her next breath she whisked his attention to other matters. She handed a letter to him.

"Be a good soul and mail this for me," she said. "And strawberries, Mr. B. Don't forget the strawberries. If they got any sets left, bring home a dozen or so. We'll grow 'em as big as pullet eggs. That Dakota sun ought to be good for something. We'll eat 'em fresh with cream and later I'll make strawberry jam that'll

look like melted rubies or the blood of a young queen."
I thought *I* had an imagination? Hers put mine to
shame.

The next morning, Mr. B. and I waved ourselves out
of the yard and began our journey to Red River. "You
two will have a chance to get truly acquainted" Belle
called to me. Quick as she was to wrath, she was just
as quick to forget harsh words.

I waited for the acquaintanceship to commence. As
with everything Mr. B. tackled, it was not to be fool-
ishly rushed into. We rode together a long while, Mr.
B. sighting carefully down the tips of Sorry's ears as a
sharpshooter might sight down a rifle barrel before he
said to me, "Belle means no harm. It's not that she's
selfish or doesn't want you and TJ to go to school."

"No, sir," I agreed.

"Things haven't gone as we planned since our arrival in the Territory, Willie. Belle wants so much out
of life, you see. And so soon."

"Yes, sir. A white house with pillars and a front
door with lots of stained glass in it."

"She told you that?"

"As we drove out to House Place on that very first
morning."

"Belle loves nice things. Pretty things. A house of
tin and logs and sod . . . well, it wasn't what she had
in mind. She craves things that please the eye and
startle the neighbors."

"I know, sir." He wanted me to like her. Maybe
even to love her. I wanted to, but it seemed a risky
business, after what I had learned from life. But to
soothe his fears I added, "Don't worry, sir. I understand. Things will be all right."

The outline of Red River appeared on the horizon
and diverted my attention from Belle. My heart began
to jump in my chest like a frog in a jar. *It's going to
look like Tipton,* I told myself. Looking on such a
place again would make me feel like a member of the
human race once more. How else could I account for
the blow to my brisket when I got my first closeup look
at Red River?

A row of tacky, unpainted, false-front buildings faced each other from opposite sides of a rutted street like gunfighters in a penny-dreadful novel. There was among that motley collection a saloon called the Pastime, a dry goods store that was also the post office, a livery stable, and a tiny shop that sold women's hats and went out of business before I ever got back to Red River a second time. Behind all that was an assortment of homes and shacks, many painted the same horrible yellow-brown color. The paint, I learned later, had been bought up cheap from the railroad.

Because it was May and because it was Saturday, the rutted street was filled with people. Dogs barked and children fled like bandits through a forest of grownups' and horses' legs. *Will he be here?* I wondered, and was annoyed to think I cared.

We had hardly alighted from July's old wagon before a voice boomed in my ear and I looked up to see a huge and hearty woman descending upon us like a freight train. She was flanked on either side by a pair of white-haired girls who could only have been her daughters.

"Ya! Mister Bannerman!" she roared in a hearty Norwegian accent. "I been lookin' for you! Ya! And the missus, too! Where is the missus?"

"Good morning, Mrs. Gunderson," Mr. B. answered, not as poleaxed as I was. "Belle did not come with me today. But here—here is someone I want you to meet—and your daughters, too." He cupped the pointy end of my elbow in his palm and steered me forward like a hard-to-manage vehicle.

"Ya, ya?" Mrs. Gunderson cried, surveying me with blue eyes that were shrewd but not exactly unkind.

"This is my niece, Mrs. Gunderson. This is Willie. Willie has come to live with Belle and me. She'll attend school this fall with Kaia and Lempii." Kaia and Lempii watched me like two hungry cats watch a solitary mouse.

Mrs. Gunderson reached for me with a large, sunbrowned hand. She clamped my upper arm in a firm grip. She squeezed, as the witch must have squeezed the pitiful twigs Gretel stuck through the bars of her cage. "Poor little goose needs the corn, don't she?" she bellowed, showing many handsome white teeth. Her daughters, on cue, began to giggle behind their hands. I felt exceedingly warm.

"Wil-leee!" one of them squealed. "Wil-leee!" Not even when Sue Buncher had hollered after me had my name sounded so silly. Kaia, the taller of the two, studied me with cheery malice, but I imagined that there was the shadow of apology in the eyes of the other girl.

Having thus speculated on the condition of my nutrition, Mrs. Gunderson's glance became unaccountably tender. "It will be good for your wife, mister, to have this niece. Won't take the place of the boy, but it will help. Ya, it will help." Then, with the roar of a train leaving the station, Mrs. Gunderson pulled away, crying over her shoulder as she departed, "And don't forget the *pa-a-a-rty!* All day long. The Fourth of July, at the bonanza farm. It will surely lift the spirits of the missus!" The Gundersons disappeared in the crowd and left me to ponder not the last remark but the one just before: Won't take the place of the boy. . . .

I trailed witlessly after Mr. B. The episode had left me in no way prepared to find myself eyeball to eyeball (except that mine were higher because I was so much taller) with the person who had lately been on my mind.

Has he shrunk? I wondered. *Or have I grown another two inches in the past six months?* When was my poor galloping carcass ever going to settle down, put meat on its frail bones, begin to look like that of a normal human female?

He wanted desperately to speak. Urgency lighted those pale exile's eyes. His mouth shaped some words: *Hello. I know you. You don't belong either. What is your name? Mine is . . .* Is that what he intended? All that came out was a muffled something in a tongue I did not understand. He knew no English. I knew no Finn.

There was nothing to do but propel myself furiously after Mr. B.

At the post office Mr. B. picked up three pieces of mail and handed me the envelope Bell had given him. He gave me three pennies. "Buy a stamp for this and mail it, would you, Willie?" he asked. I did, and scrutinized the address, scribed in Belle's fine and spidery writing: *Acme Travel Agency and Tours, New York, N. Y.*

"Is Belle planning a trip?" I asked.

Mr. B. smiled. "No, I don't think so. But she says no one writes to her. So she sends for things—travel information, catalogs, lists of books she doesn't really want to read. Just to get something in the mail." It seemed a strange hobby to me, but Mr. B., unperturbed, continued his purchase of garden seeds. Then came warm mittens and heavy shoes for the trips TJ and I would make to school. Two lunch boxes, a pair of notebooks, an assortment of pencils, and we were finished. When everything had been paid for, Mr. B. counted the remainder of his funds into his palm. "Just enough left over to buy strawberry sets for Belle," he said. "Twenty-five cents apiece, but a dozen would please her so much."

"To make jam that looks like melted rubies or the blood of a young queen," I reminded him.

He smiled. "She likes her language as she likes her clothes—colorful."

The clerk dampened the strawberry sets, withered brownish clumps, wrapped them in brown butcher's paper, and tied the package with string.

But Belle was abashed when he put the parcel into her hands. "I'm forever yearning after the frivolous, ain't I, Mr. B.?" she lamented. "Pomegranates. Avocadoes. Persimmons. Fruits of a southern sun. I forget, somehow, that this is Dakota Territory."

"I got them partly for Willie," Mr. B. lied, "if that will make you feel better. Perhaps strawberries and cream will put some pounds on her. Mrs. Gunderson allowed to me that she looks like a goose that needs some corn."

Belle was immediately indignant. She seized me by my bony shoulders and clapped me, astonished, against her own whip-thin self. "Pshaw! Don't people know you can't put fat on a thoroughbred? Willie looks fine just the way she is."

I gasped for air. "She had something else to say, Belle."

"What?"

"There's going to be a party. On the Fourth of July. At the bonanza farm."

She hugged me harder. "Wheee! Now ain't that just exactly the kind of news I needed to hear! Why, luv, we'll dance all night and way into the morning!" And by way of practicing for that marathon she whirled me madly around Herschvogel until TJ got jealous and demanded a dance of his own.

As nights went, that was one of TJ's fussier. He took more than his share of the covers and stole better than his half of the pallet. Below, Belle and Mr. B. stirred in their great brass boat. I stared at the ceiling that loomed an arm's length over my head. Mice rustled above the boards and a rain of dirt loosened by their feet sprinkled across the quilt.

It had been a mixed-up day. "Won't take the place of the boy" . . . the urgency of a pair of lonesome gray eyes . . . "Wil-leee, Wil-leee" . . . they may have been female but they were no more like me than apples are like onions. . . .

And how's a girl named Willie supposed to feel anyhow? I wondered. I placed each palm over a certain spot on either side of my chest. Yes. Still there. Buds about to flower. Breasts. I wasn't ready, either. Had this already happened to Beth Ellen? Had it *ever* happened to Louisa May Alcott, so noble and good? Or to Pauline Cushman, under her major's uniform? Maybe only to me?

The notion caused me pain. Only the pain was not located on the unsmooth surface of my bony chest. It was buried deep in the interior of me, close beside the cold, round, hard turtle that I called my heart.

9

Once Mr. B. had turned over the prairie sod—which was black and stringy with grassroots and which became hard as firebrick once it'd been laid face-up to the stern Dakota sun—we all began to hack at it with hoes and shovels. That earth almost refused to be subdued, but when we'd done the best we could, July fashioned us a planting bar from a stick sharpened to a dagger point on one end.

"Guaranteed to save one of you an ache in the back," he said, holding it out to Belle. "Now who gets to use the stick and who gets to put the seeds in the hole and tamp them down?"

"TJ can put the seeds in," Belle decreed, "since he's closer to the ground to start with." TJ crept along on hands and knees, cross-eyed with concentration, while Belle made holes and I tamped them over with my bare heel. When peas, beans, squash, rutabagas, onions, parsnips, and carrots had been planted, we set out potato eyes. The strawberries had already been planted and mulched with old straw cleaned from the barn.

"And ain't we going to feel rich," Belle dreamed, "with all these edibles stashed away for the winter? Oh, the stews we won't have, gravies thick as pudding, chock-full of stuff grown right here at the Bannerman empire!"

TJ screwed up his face. "I don't much care for stew," he said, being as tactful as he could. "Truth to tell, ain't never liked the stuff. Once I had to stand in the corner all night because I wouldn't eat my stew."

Belle poked sassily at TJ's rear end with the planting bar. "You are going to love Belle Bannerman's stew," she insisted. "Nobody makes mulligan like an Irish woman, of which I am undoubtedly the grandest!" She favored him with a sly wink and I knew that even if TJ hated stew as much as he had in Tennessee, he'd just the same eat Belle's. TJ was in love. People do strange things for love.

When we had finished our planting Belle shaded her eyes and stared at the sky. "Do you know what sort of a day this is?" she asked.

TJ shaded his eyes too and stared up as though he expected the answer to be written in the spring blueness. "What kind?"

"This is a go to the Red River and gather moss agates kind of day, that's what. Want to come along?"

Belle folded some cold biscuits into a napkin, filled a mason jar with cold coffee, and off we set. We walked south across the prairie, which seemed as flat to me as the top of a table, until the earth began to slope gradually toward the Red River. We threaded our way through low shrubbery, chokecherry and buffaloberry and currant, until we found ourselves on a wide, sandy beach. "We surely must've got turned around somehow," I said, for I could see that the river flowed north. I turned around: no, east was still in the east, the west was still west.

Belle laughed. "Even the river in Dakota Territory is contrary," she said. "Let the Mississippi and the Missouri and the Platte flow downhill to the Gulf—the Red decided to flow uphill into Canada. The only river on the continent with a mind of its own—a river after my own heart!"

We sifted the smooth river sand through our fingers as Belle showed us how to do, coming now and then upon a smooth, round, common-looking pebble. But washed in the water, as she demonstrated for us, and polished on a cloth, there emerged from the milky surface of the moss agates such scenes as you could not imagine: moonscapes, visions of tawny meadows and unscalable cliffs, fire-tortured trees, buried in silica and quartz. TJ found a stone that bore the image of a wild-haired woman; I found one that showed me the view I'd seen from the Widow Wilson's hillside.

When we had all filled our pockets, Belle spread out biscuits and cold coffee on the hem of her skirt. "Willie," she mused, "have you ever had the feeling you haven't found the place yet you were meant to be? I mean, I see such places when I study the moss agates. Places maybe not found on any map. . . ."

I denied any such uncertainty. "Why, no, ma'am. It pleasures me just to be right here with you in Dakota Territory. Whyever would I want to be someplace else?"

"Once I dreamed of a field of blue butterflies," she said. "I caught some in my hat. They were lovely and fragile as a hatful of wishes."

"I don't think you're apt to find such things in the Territory," I said. She trailed her fingers through the sand toward my own, teased my knuckles with her fingertips.

"Know what else, Willie?"

"No, what?"

"You're older, my girl, than I'll ever be. Wise, old, sensible Willie."

By the middle of June, the peas and beans had come up out of the ground like ladies' bent hairpins, and the sweet corn had appeared as rows of tiny green rabbit ears. When the weather warmed and got dry, we watered each plant by hand with a dipperful of water from a bucket we'd carried from the creek. In the strawberry bed, runners sent bright green messages in all directions and began to show blossoms here and there. It was then the Snowbird decided to do me a favor.

Day after day I had tugged and hauled on her halter. Day after day she resisted as elegantly as ever. Finally, I gave up. "You want it this way?" I asked. "Fine. I am not a fool who will invite a rattlesnake to dinner. I am also not going to beg and plead with you anymore." I unclipped the rope from the halter. You picked the wrong person, Mr. B., I would tell him. To July I would confess: I wasn't up to the job. The Snowbird broke me; it wasn't the other way around.

I marched toward the corral gate. The latch Mr. B. had made from wood and leather was hard to manage and a fly buzzed against my arm. It was morning but the sky was already bleached white by heat. I was hot and cross and mean. The fly persisted; I turned to deliver it a deadly whack. Only it was not a fly on my arm. It was the Snowbird, nuzzling my elbow.

"You pesky varmint," I snuffled. "You just about did me in!" I hugged her silver face against my chest, then clipped the rope onto the halter and led her across the yard to House Place. I knocked on the door.

"Got a surprise," I announced to Mr. B., and stepped aside. The Snowbird lowered her eyes demurely.

He was more relieved than I was. "You finally did it, Willie. I was just about ready to give up on you."

"Jeezel beezel, Willie," TJ exclaimed, "now you can lead her anywhere."

Belle craned her head out the door. "I never doubted you for a minute, Willie," she told me. But she was too busy with her sewing to pay my victory much mind. The morning after she'd gotten the news about the party, she'd begun to scramble through the trunk at the end of her bed. Dresses of every gypsy hue spilled out of it or were tossed willy-nilly all around the room. Dresses of watered silk or crisp taffeta; dresses of wool and dresses of linen; dresses green and burgundy and yellow and every shade in between; dresses decorated and dresses plain.

"I got to have something to wear that'll make an impression," Belle told me.

"I'm impressed and you ain't even wearing any of 'em," I allowed.

"I got to have something wonderful and downright unforgettable," she insisted, and dragged forth a dress of rose-colored silk. It was tolerably wrinkled, but she peeled off her cambric housedress and jumped into it. She buttoned the rose silk to her neck, smoothed it across her bosom, and surveyed herself critically in the mirror.

"What do you think, Willie?"

"You look like a torch," I admitted. And she did—a regular conflagration of rose silk and bonfire hair. "Somebody's going to want to put you out," I warned. I had only to remember Mrs. Gunderson's no-nonsense blue eyes or Mr. Rich's pious smile to be sure of that.

"You really think so?" Belle beamed. If I had meant to dissuade her I had not been successful. "Sounds like just the ticket to me. But I'm thinner than when we came out here. I'll take a tuck here and there. It should fit to a fare-thee-well."

I considered my own image in her mirror. Mine was still, after seven months in the Territory, a sparsely thatched, narrow-eyed bandit face off a "Wanted" poster. Actually, I looked worse, not better, than when we'd arrived in the Territory. My hair, which had been painfully brief then but was a uniform degree of ugly, now sprouted from my scalp in irregular clumps. What appeared to be two spikey horns now grew directly above my eyebrows and a pair of long, raggedy spaniel's ears attempted to cover my human ones.

But a decent dress to wear might help my situation. I nipped up the ladder into our sleeping loft and hauled Mama's dress of periwinkle blue out of Papa's valise, scattering bits of paper as I did so. I threw it down onto the kitchen floor ahead of me and Belle shook it out.

"Lovely color, Willie!" she observed. "Might even look good on you."

In the next two days, Belle detached bodice from skirt, sleeves from bodice, took in darts, moved seams inward, created a garment that more or less conformed to the carcass it was intended to fit. The only thing that did not need to be altered was the hem: already I was as tall as Mama had been.

"But my hair," I groaned. "I still look like a bank robber!"

"Don't worry, luv," Belle said. "I got a curling iron hid away somewhere. Come the day of the party we will crimp you up so even the Snowbird won't know you."

"You sure?"

"Law! Don't you know I can do anything I say I can do?" She pinched my cheek gently. I would have to trust her and hope for the best.

But that night, as soon as I was sure TJ was asleep, I sat up on our pallet. I fished the broken-handled mirror out from where I'd hid it under my pillow. I peered hopefully into it, but it was too dark to see much of anything except two suspicious eyes staring back at me. Quite enough, however, to make me wish I'd never cut off my only decent feature, as Mrs. Rich had called my long brown hair. Even a dress of periwinkle blue could not make up for the crime I had committed against myself.

"Lordy, Lordy," I whispered, "don't I just wish I was pretty." Such a vain notion had never before occurred to me. "I wish I looked like Belle. I wish . . ."

TJ rose up off his half of the pallet, his own eyes a pair of outraged stars in the attic dimness. "Well, you don't," he informed me crisply. "You ain't beautiful and you ain't never going to be. Now lay down and let me get some sleep." As though tomorrow he would be hitched to July's wagon and would have to pull it all the way to the bonanza farm himself.

I am the sort of person who never cries. Never. Not when Mama and Papa died. Not when we had boarded that train in Tipton to leave our home forever. Now, tears as surprising as some sin I never meant to commit leaped out of my eyes and spilled down my cheeks. I leaned my forehead on my bent-up knees and wept buckets and barrels and broomhandles.

"Willie, Willie," TJ warned, "I think your eyes has sprung a leak." He crept close and delivered remorseful pat-pat-pats to the top of my shorn head. His fingers were still syrupy from the cornbread we'd eaten for supper and my forlorn mop stuck to them like flies to flypaper.

"Jeezel beezel, Willie," he groaned. "It don't matter a pea particle to me if you ain't beautiful. Not really."

I howled louder. "You are going to be better than beautiful," he insisted. "You said so your own self. Said you were going to be famous. That's better. For you, anyways. Especially since there ain't much chance of you being good-looking anyhow."

I lay down. Tears ran into my ears. "Go to sleep, TJ," I begged. "Stop. Desist. Quit. Your cures are worse than my disease." He folded me like something breakable against his sharp pigeon breast and, for the first time in memory, I was asleep before he was.

10

The day of the party arrived before I was ready. Not that it mattered: Belle was ready enough for all of us. She braided her red hair into a queen's crown, rouged her cheeks until they gleamed like votive lights, donned that torch of a dress, laced up her yellow leather shoes, and happily scandalized our eyes.

Only when all that had been accomplished was it my turn. She whipped out the curling iron, rescued from its hiding place in the bottom of her trunk. She stuck it headfirst into the chimney of a lighted kerosene lamp and when the wand was hot, plucked it out, opened its scissors jaws, and clamped them enthusiastically around wads of my rebellious hair. Soon House Place was perfumed with the stench of my overcooked tresses.

"Ain't those Gunderson girls going to be green as grass when they see you!" Belle chortled. It was, truth to tell, a delicious thought. But when I saw my wavy reflection in the yellow mirror I decided they would probably not fall down in fits of envy. On the other hand, my convict's countenance had been traded for that of a curly-haired page from King Arthur's court. The Bannermans had carried the king's colors into battle for centuries—and I was living testimony to the fact.

"Now leap like a lizard into that dress of your ma's," Belle directed when she had completed the torture of my hair. "Should fit you to perfection, if I do say so myself." She was right, and if your taste runs to fence posts turned out in gowns of periwinkle blue, then I was a success. Even TJ admitted it.

"I seen you look a lot worse, Willie."

The splendiferous possibilities of the coming event inspired July to pour water over his peppersalt curls, which he then combed with his fingers. He ministered to his hands in such a way that the half-moons of soil beneath his nails mellowed to grayness. We were ready for the party. Except for one small detail.

"I sure hate to leave the Snowbird here," I fumed. "What if it's like July says, that the Sioux think white's a good luck color? They might come and snatch her off while we're gone."

"Shoo!" Belle declared. "We'll take her right along with us! The Bird can trot along beside Fanny and it'll be good exercise for her." So we set out, TJ and July and me in the back of the wagon, seeing to it that the baskets of fried prairie chicken, the biscuits, and the cake stayed upright, while Belle and Mr. B. sat on the wagon bench like royalty.

When we arrived at the bonanza farm, an imposing pillared white house three stories tall with many out-buildings spread in all directions, Mr. B. unhitched Fanny and tied her apart from the other wagons so that she could graze easily and the Snowbird would not attract undue attention. Inside the largest of the barns, which had been swept clean and was newly white-washed, tables stretched hither and yon, heaped with pies and hams and more fried chicken. The rafters overhead were hung with loops of curly paper in red and blue and white. Kegs of root beer and jugs of lemonade were placed at the end of each table.

And it became clear what Belle had in mind.

When she sailed into that barn, filled with people of all sizes and shapes and ages, conversation came to a standstill. Heads turned. Men's gazes were admiring, women's slanty-eyed and suspicious. Belle toured their ranks like a queen on an official mission: an imperious, tinkling laugh here, a gliding swoop past some jealous wife there. She soon was lost to my sight and not recovered until two hours later when, with my sixth chicken wing poised midway to my mouth, she hissed in my ear, "I got something to show you, Willie! Hurry! You can eat chicken anytime!"

She pulled me along, out of the barn, through a field of wild mustard to the large, white, many-pillared house. "You've got to see what it looks like in there," she whispered. "Willie, you won't believe it. I hardly did myself."

"You mean you been in there, Belle? Who invited you?"

"I invited myself."

"You can't just go walking into other folks' houses, Belle." I stopped on the porch, nervous as a cat in a roomful of rockers.

"Ain't nobody living there right now," she sniffed airily. "Those folks only come out to the Territory every now and then, with their ritzy friends from the East. This place is run by a manager, Willie. Those bankers and brokers and business types don't mess their hands laboring on a place like this."

One door was not enough for a house the likes of that one: it had two, each with a pane of oval glass, and overhead was a transom spanning both made of stained glass in the sweetest colors seen this side of paradise. Belle put her hand on the knob, opened the door on the right, and we stepped inside. She beckoned to me.

"Belle, I don't think this is a very good idea," I allowed. But I followed her just the same.

The house was hushed and cool. The mellow tinkle of a wind chime came from a distant room. Having left the barn and stepped into this place, we became travelers in a foreign land. The walls surrounding us were papered in velvet and gilt. The carpets were plum and to have called the furniture overstuffed would not have done it justice.

We padded, like burglars, from room to room. The dining room was set with crystal and silver and lace for those who dined there but twice a year. The library was shelved with books, floor to ceiling, waiting to be read. Belle motioned me to the stairs leading to the floors above.

"Let's not go up there, Belle. It ain't right."

She stood on the landing, six steps above me. To her left was a small, round window of stained glass in designs of roses and vines and grapes. The colored light, in palest shades of rose and green and blue, filtered across her white face.

"I want it all, Willie."

"All what, Belle?"

"This." She tapped the mahogany balustrade. "These carpets. All this gilt and glass and gold. The good things. I want all of them." She raised one hand to finger the tiny blue lapel watch at her shoulder.

"Mr. B.'s just starting out, Belle. Give him time. He hasn't the money and the partners and the connections these bonanza farmers do." Papa had been in business. I knew about such things.

She stared down but did not see me. If envy comes in colors, they must be the bonny blues and mellow greens and dusty roses of prairie sunlight filtered through a piece of stained glass in a rich man's house. I grabbed her hand. "C'mon, Belle, this is crazy. We been here too long already. Someone'll catch us sure." She allowed me to steer her out the door and let me close it behind us. But I knew by the way she marched ahead of me through the wild mustard, ramrod-straight, that I had said nothing to change her way of thinking. She began to hum, sweetly and off-key.

> I know where I'm going and I know who's going with me,
> But I would leave it all for my handsome, winsome Johnnie. . . .

When the dancing started in the evening, after the barn was filled with smoky haze and everyone was acting like loving kin to each other from a long time back, Belle and Mr. B. began to whirl madly around and around. Belle tossed her head back, her crown began to come askew, her eyes were glittery with delight. I found myself a spot in the corner, out of sight of Kaia and Lempii across the room, and stuck my twenty-seventh chicken wing into my mouth.

"Can . . . will . . . you dance?" a voice inquired in my ear. The words were uttered in a manner most careful, halting and precise. Either the speaker did not know how to talk or wasn't sure how to dance, I decided. But when I turned around, at least his eyes seemed only a little lower this time than mine. Either he'd grown or I'd stopped.

I didn't know how to dance a step, but without saying yea or nay to his invitation, I placed one hand on his shoulder and the other in his broad, cool paw and we galumphed furiously around the room like everyone else. He didn't know how to dance either and I heard gasps of amazement as we ricocheted through the crowd.

"I . . . saw . . . her," he panted in my ear. His accent was heavy, but I could make out what he said. "Your . . . horse. The silver filly. You . . . are . . . lucky."

"It depends," I panted back.

"Depends . . . ?"

"I doubt she'll ever be much good behind a plow," I said, denying luck of any kind.

"But she'll be . . . fine . . . for dreaming on."

A dreamer meets a dreamer. Only another dreamer would have untangled my denial. I searched his face, hoping to see something else written there, and was fetched into a pair of cool, gray eyes. His lashes were thick, like tiny golden brushes. When the music changed and a waltz commenced, the whirling crowd plastered us together from clavicle to knee.

Except for TJ, I'd never been so close to a human being in my life—and him only when it'd been my intent to keep him from committing some rash act we'd both be sorry for. This other closeness caused a peculiar tickle in my midsection that made me wonder if I hadn't eaten a few too many chicken wings—a condition not improved when I caught a baleful glare from Kaia Gunderson out of the corner of my eye. Then the

music stopped and the dance was over. That other
dreamer gave my hand a quick squeeze and vanished
into the crowd.

Going home, the night was warm. The new moon
hung, thin as the skin over an old scar, on the western
horizon. TJ and I lay on the straw in the back of the
wagon. "Feel my stomach," TJ invited proudly. "It's
just like a drum."

I patted that drum: inside, drumsticks and ham
slices and chocolate cake beat a lively tune. Later, I
knew, he would be sicker than a poisoned pup and I
would have to hold his head. With a sigh, he curled
himself into my arms, smelling sweetly of root beer and
sweat.

"Willie, you was . . . was practically pretty tonight,"
he yawned.

It was true. I'd felt it myself. Might be the only time,
though. Only three days ago to be pretty had seemed
genuinely important; now it did not seem to matter
very much. I raised myself on one elbow and peered
over the side of the wagon.

In the faint light, the Snowbird loomed as silent and
silver as a ghost. Odd: I could not quite hear the
sound of her hoofbeats on the earth. She seemed to
float beside the wagon, a few inches off the ground.
She turned her silver face to mine. I could see the scar
of the thin moon reflected in her amazed black eyes.

I lay back and closed my own, *Willie, your parts are
coming together,* that other Willie told me. *One at a
time. Heart hooked back to head. Liver to spleen. It all
takes time. Something you got lots of.*

11

He was packed like a sausage into the space allowed by his desk, knees doubled under his chin, hands knotted on the wooden slab in front of him. He kept his pale eyes averted from mine. His towheaded twin sisters were there, not to mention the Gunderson girls, a pair of robust corn maidens out of a Nordic fairy tale. I was taller than anyone in the room. Including the teacher. But then, wasn't I taller than almost anyone in the Territory with the possible exception of Mr. B.?

"My name is Miss Pratt," the teacher informed us. "Miss Mercy Pratt, lately from the Hoosier state of Indiana, and this is my first year in the Territory of Dakota." Now some people look like ordinary objects you are familiar with: barrels, trees, whips, ships. Miss Pratt was a button. Not more than five feet tall and composed entirely of buttons: brown shoe-button eyes, a quirky button mouth, a sunburned, peeling button for a nose.

"We are going to be doing some sharing and caring in this little room," she said, making a grand gesture that included us all. "I will be teaching you some things and you will teach me a few things and together we will sail away on that wonderful ship called Learning."

Well. Miss Abercrombie in Tipton hadn't liked learning any more than she relished children. Most particularly she had disliked me. She said I was snippety and my imagination ran to the impossible. Papa said it was not such a bad way to be, but, as with other judgments he passed on me, did not trouble to explain himself further. If Button Person wanted to sail away on a ship called Learning, well, then I was plenty ready to hop on board.

We'd only been in school a scarce two weeks before TJ distracted me with dire predictions of events to come. "That Kaia," he warned. "She don't care much for you, Willie. I seen her watching you and if looks was leprosy your nose would be falling off this minute."

"I know all about it," I said. "It's on account of she's jealous."

"Of what? Why'd any girl take it into her head to be jealous of you? Besides, she don't even know you. How can anybody hate a person they don't even know?"

"It's because of that immigrant boy. Urho Kiiskaala."

"You mean she don't know him either?"

"No, dopey. I mean Kaia likes him. Loves him, who knows? Who cares? Only she thinks he likes me."

"You? Naw. He don't know you're alive."

I knew otherwise, of course. When Miss Pratt asked me to help Urho with his letters, just as I helped TJ, right there in the classroom while she tended to the other students, I saw no reason not to oblige.

"B . . . B . . . B . . . b . . . b . . . b," I instructed them both to write in their copybooks. "Which can mean bee. ZZZZzzzz." I drew a picture of a bee, complete with stripes. "Or I got to *be* going home now. B . . . b . . . now, you both got that?" Urho mouthed the letters after me, carefully and slowly, eyes fastened on mine as though I harbored deep down some precious secret of life. TJ, of course, saw no need to apply himself so earnestly.

Urho traced the letters in his copybook with a small child's diligence. His knuckles were raw and unwashed, his fingernails black and broken. Mr. B. said the Kiiskaalas possessed only a shovel for planting, that they harvested their scant plot of potatoes by hand. But those pale clear holes in Urho's face, windows more transparent even than TJ's violet ones, yearned toward me with trust and conviction in my powers.

I knew the time I spent with Urho would carry a price tag. TJ and I were lollygagging down the dry creek bed that separated our quarter section of land from the bonanza farm, the low walls of which rose on either side of us like the sides of a shallow dish, when Kaia appeared suddenly on the rim of that dish, blocking out the sun, arms akimbo, mouth a stern and forbidding slash in her outraged face.

"The Finn," she hissed at me, "he ain't for you. He's one of us. An immigrant like Lempii and me. Like most of us here in the Territory." Lempii stood behind Kaia and plucked at her sister's sleeve.

I made no comment. For once. "He's our kind," she rushed on, breathless with fury. "He's got nothing in common with the likes of you or that crazy lady you live with."

It was the first time I'd heard Belle called crazy. "She ain't neither," TJ hollered. "She loves us and she ain't crazy!" For TJ, love made all things understandable. It did not matter to Kaia, however: she continued to glare down on me, cornflower eyes fierce and full of business. I knew she was fixing to clobber me. What I didn't know was when.

She clearly mistook my silence for insolence and made a leap off the bank to dispatch me a mighty whack alongside my head. I went to my knees without a peep. Kaia was on top of me before my eyes cleared and all I could do was cover my face and hope I didn't get scratched to pieces.

From somewhere above my folded arms I heard a shrill squeal; Kaia rolled off me as suddenly as she had got me down. I opened one eye to see TJ fly off the bank himself, arms and legs whirling like windmill blades late for work. He flailed and smacked and whacked in every direction like an old she-bear defending a helpless cub.

"TJ, TJ!" I hollered. "It's all right. Quit. Cease. Desist." I looped my arms around his banshee body and in the fracas he laid a proper one across my left eyebrow.

"She don't need to say that about Belle!" TJ cried. "Belle ain't crazy. Belle's good to us." *Ah*. So he was not defending me, after all. It was Belle's honor that motivated him.

I held onto him long enough for Kaia to scramble up the embankment. No more was she the gold corn maiden from a fable: her yellow hair was tangled and full of burrs. She spat dirt out of her mouth and it appeared to me she might've chipped a front tooth. Overall, she had been poleaxed.

"You keep that little varmint away from me!" she screeched. "He just tried to kill me, that's what he tried to do! Tried to kill me!"

I narrowed my eyes at her. "You got to be awful careful around TJ," I said. "He's got the strength of ten when riled. You know how it is with folks that are . . ." I made descriptive circles around my ear. She thought Belle was the crazy one? I looked down at TJ; he slavered and barked loudly three times. "Even at home, see, we have to be real careful around him. Tsk, tsk. Such a temperamental little tyke."

Kaia backed off from the rim of the ditch. Lempii grinned at me to let me know she thought she understood what I was up to. "He ain't really . . ." (more descriptive ear circles) ". . . is he?"

I was about to say no when it occurred to me I might need insurance for the future. "We-e-e-l-l-l," I temporized, "I sure wouldn't take any liberties around him, if I was you. Just be ver-r-r-y careful."

Lempii too leaped away from the edge of the bank and galloped, exclaiming in Norwegian, after her sister. "Good riddance," TJ said.

Before we arrived at House Place, we combed our hair with our fingers, rubbed spit on our cheeks and scrubbed them as clean as such efforts would permit. The knot over my eye felt big as a squash.

"Do I look normal?"

"Normal as you ever will, I reckon," TJ said.

"Good Lord Amighty, what happened to the two of

you?" Belle wanted to know the minute she spied us. "You look like something the cat dragged through a knothole."

"We had a fight," TJ announced, pleased to be the bearer of bad news.

"A fight? You're brother and sister, one of you big and the other one little. What can there be to fight about?"

"Oh, we didn't fight with each other. Willie's got this here boyfriend and another girl likes him, too. She cleaned Willie's clock. Mighta been worse, but I stepped in and saved her."

"Ah. A boyfriend." The tone of her voice made it impossible for me to decide whether she was pleased or aggravated. "Why didn't I guess? A girl gets to be a certain age it's all she seems to think about. She's been in the Territory less than a year and already got herself a man."

"He ain't a man," TJ corrected. "Only a boy. An imm'grunt boy."

"One of our Scandinavian neighbors, I take it," put in Mr. B. "You could do worse than one of those hard-working Gunderson boys."

"His name's Urho Kiiskaala and he's Finn," I said, feeling like a criminal making a confession. "Only he ain't my boyfriend. I don't aim to trade or deal in boyfriends. Not for a long time. Maybe ever. Miss Pratt asked me to help him learn his letters is all, same's I help TJ. Didn't see any harm in the idea at the time."

"Miss Pratt this and Miss Pratt that," Belle sighed. Had I talked about Miss Pratt so much she had to use such a tone of voice?

At supper, when July got wind of the boyfriend business, he pretended no surprise at all. "Sure, you'll be married and gone before we know it," he predicted. "Gals ain't content until they got some poor dude trussed and tied and helpless as a pig headed for the roasting pit."

"Your elegant description does you justice," Belle

told him. "But not all gals want to be married. Maybe Willie's one of 'em. Ain't no crime, you know."

I raised my lashes enough to sneak a quick peek at Mr. B. He was thoughtfully moving food from one place to another around his plate as though something strange had happened to the taste of it.

Two days later I pawed and clawed my way through the hundreds of bits and scraps and pieces of paper, those corners of old envelopes, snippets of copybook pages, backs of bills of lading that languished at the bottom of Papa's valise. That is where I had hidden my piece of melted typeset after our arrival in the Territory. Now I retrieved it, wrapped it in the corner of my handkerchief, tied a knot to secure it, and pinned the whole affair to the inside of the pocket in my skirt. I did not aim to lose such a precious talisman should Kaia decide to turn me end-over-teakettle again in some prairie ditch.

Through the long afternoon, that reminder lay heavy on my thigh. The blood and bones and brains of William and Anna Bannerman, to whom I owed a debt not yet paid. Even if I'd wanted to forget, that other Willie would never let me.

The problem was, I was a miser and hoarder of words. They fell out of my head like moths shaken out of an old coat: *It isn't fit, Harold Rich, a girl her age should be sleeping with a brother. . . . Anna, if I don't do this now, tell what I've found out, let all Tipton County know the truth, I'm no different from any of the others. . . . That Willie; a strange girl—lucky it is they have Thomas Jefferson, who is so nice and ordinary . . .* preserved scribblings without beginnings, middles, or ends. And it looked like I might be a scribbler the rest of my life.

"I will surely be pleased to help you straighten up, Miss Pratt," I said. She was the only one who might have a solution to my dilemma. I was past fourteen years of age; I couldn't wait forever to get started.

"Now isn't that precious of you, Willie!" Miss Pratt

spoke in extremes and exclamations. "But I can manage alone! I expect you got chores to do at home!"

"No, ma'am. Not tonight. That is to say, TJ offered to do 'em for me. Ain't that much to do now that we got the hay all put up. Give a bit of grain to the Snowbird. Feed the hens and their rooster. Gather up the few eggs might've got laid during the day. Thing is, Miss Pratt, I got to speak to you about a problem."

"Why, of course, Willie!"

"Miss Pratt, I promised my mother and my father that I would do them proud someday. I promised I would carry on ideas they believed in, that I would do some dreaming and some telling."

My words arrested Miss Pratt in her tracks. She made a platform of her laced fingers and laid her chin upon it. "Willie! How marvelous! It's like poetry: dreaming and telling! My, Mr. Bannerman and your mother must be ever so pleased with you!"

"Oh, they are not my parents, those people I am living with now," I said. "Mr. B., he's my father's brother. My uncle. Mama and Papa were killed back in Tipton County, Tennessee, more than a year ago. Wash McDermott and his boys set a torch to Papa's newspaper and both my parents died in the blaze." The words had gotten very easy to say.

For once, Miss Pratt was too stunned to scribe exclamation points in the air with her voice. "Willie, I am sorry. I had no idea. . . ."

"Don't fret over it," I said. I pulled on my hair. It did not quite cover my earlobes. "Miss Pratt, I want to be a writer. I want to write books. Only I don't know how to commence."

Miss Pratt unfolded her laced fingers and hugged her pink cheeks between her palms. "Now, Willie, didn't I just know you were different? The minute you walked through that door, why, I knew right off you were special!" Sure she did. How many other almost-bald-headed girls did she have in her school? "Truly, Willie, you are a mercurial person!"

"Oh, no," I objected, feeling warm. "I'm solid as a rock."

"Dear, it was a compliment."

"Oh." It was like those things Papa used to say about me, without ever explaining what he meant. I galloped right on to the heart of the matter: "I have to learn how to write, Miss Pratt. Not the shaping letters part of writing; you know I know how to do that. I mean *write*. Tell a story that goes from one place to another, has beginnings and middles and ends."

Miss Pratt hopped on top of one of the benches and sat cross-legged in front of me. She chewed on her lip. "Willie, I'm not a writer myself so maybe I can't give you the kind of advice you deserve. But it seems to me that good writers are first of all good readers. They read lots of different things. Science and history and poetry and plays. Maybe if you start where some other writers have started . . ."

"TJ says I'm not old enough to write," I interrupted. "He says you got to be a lot older than I am. He's only seven. He don't know much. But what if, just this once, he's right as rainwater?"

Miss Pratt turned suddenly sly. "Now what do you think he'd say if he knew that Louisa May Alcott was only seven when she began to keep her first Journal?" Old Lou-ezza Who-ezza! TJ would never believe it. He'd be sure I was lying.

"Just because a person is eight or ten or twelve does not mean that person has nothing to say. What is said at twenty or thirty or fifty might possibly be said better—or maybe only differently. But you have to start somewhere. Sometime. And maybe little Louisa knew something important that we don't: maybe a Journal is the best place to start."

"Well, I don't have a Journal. All I got is a suitcase full of itty bitty pieces and scraps and tidbits of paper. Ideas chase each other like rabbits through my head and out again. Nothing gets truly captured."

Miss Pratt catapulted herself off the bench and skipped to her desk. "I have something here you can use," she said. "It's a ledger. I was going to use it to try to keep track of my expenses—how much it cost me to travel to Fargo last month, what I paid for some gaiters and a brooch at Red River the last time I was there. The pages have little red and blue lines running every which way, but you can ignore them."

She put the ledger in my hand. It was heavy. Its cover was blue canvas and the binding was burgundy. I would owe her more than I could ever tell. "Miss Pratt? Could this be a . . . a secret? Kaia and Lempii—even TJ—think I got strange ideas. I believe even that immigrant boy thinks I'm a little peculiar." I did not mention how I thought Belle might feel.

"Of course, Willie. It will be our secret. For as long as you want it to be."

My shadow fell ahead of me like a telegraph pole as I walked east toward House Place. Ordinarily it was the time of day to make me feel a trifle melancholy, when thoughts of that other home occurred to me. The ledger under my arm seemed to make a difference. It was heavy but, for once, my heart was light.

Just the same, I did not relish the notion of walking into House Place with my new possession and having to explain its purpose. I stopped at July's corner in the barn, knocked lightly at the door, which was askew.

"Can I leave this here?"

He blinked. "Taking up bookkeeping, I see. Going into business, I suppose? Want to be rich like certain other female persons I might mention but won't. Ain't you gals all alike?"

"Not really. But this is a secret." I tapped the blue and burgundy ledger. "Don't tell anyone."

"That you're going into business and are going to be rich?"

"No, foolish. That I'm going to be a writer. If I say so to Belle it will only fuss her up. She don't seem to think highly of Miss Pratt for some reason."

July nodded; I needed to say no more. "All right, sis. Just cut me in for part of the profits when you get to be famous and known all around the world."

"Oh, I will, I will. We'll have more swag than we can count."

"Good. On account of money don't seem to know I'm alive. And don't forget how to spell my name."

"How *do* you spell your name?"

"*J-u-l-y*. It's only got four letters. Say, you're on the dim side, ain't you, for a writer-lady?"

"Not that one. The other one. The one you said was so hard to pronounce that day you brought us out to House Place."

"It ain't got any easier since you came to the Territory, sis."

"Tell me anyway."

"Chemeliewski."

"Well. At least I know now you don't tell lies."

"You neither, I hope."

"Never," I said. "Not unless I got a good reason." I closed the door of his cubbyhole and walked across the yard to House Place. I stepped inside. It was warm and cozy and I was older.

12

" 'My spirit is too weak—mortality weighs heavily on me like unwilling sleep . . .' "

"Willie, I got something to tell you." TJ gave a grunt and shoved the cart forward. "Since you took up so chummy with that Miss Pratt, no one can make head or tail out of what you say. It's a regular caution. And my opinion is this: if you got to sleep, for Lord's sake lay down and sleep."

"That's a line from a poem by John Keats. It does not mean I am sleepy or that he was either." While TJ pushed I had the dubious honor of picking up buffalo chips for the evening fire in Herschvogel's black belly. It was a smelly pastime and the chips, some as big as dinner plates, often were covered with vermin. They wouldn't smell too good burning, either. But chips made a hot, fast fire and best of all, they were free.

"Ain't that Keats person old enough to tell his own poems? Reciting ain't exactly your big suit."

"He can't recite 'em. He's dead."

"No great loss, I'd say."

"He was only twenty-four when he passed on. In Italy. That's where he died." I threw two more dinner plates on TJ's cart and could see the poet's grave, daisy-covered, as Miss Pratt, who had seen it herself, had described it to me.

"Twenty-four. That's ancient. Dying don't matter when you're that old."

"Twenty-four ain't ancient and dying always matters to the one who's making the trip," I assured him.

"There's another famous poet buried beside him. Percy Bysshe Shelley."

"Bish, fish. What kind of people would name their own child Bish?"

"Bysshe. It was a family name, I think. Maybe something like Bannerman. Only they had titles and lots of money."

The wheelbarrow was nearly full and Belle would be waiting for us. "All I know is, Willie, I've heard enough about poetry to last me a lifetime. Why don't you learn to cook instead? At least I could do something with that. Providing it didn't taste too awful."

"I can learn to cook anytime. Miss Pratt ain't going to be around forever. I got to take advantage of her, if I want to be a writer and all."

"Give it up. Be more like Belle. That's the way ladies are supposed to be."

"What way?"

"Pretty."

"TJ, why don't you save your breath to cool your soup? I can't be like Belle. Nobody can be like somebody else. Besides, you are the very person who is all the time reminding me that I am not going to be pretty under any condition."

TJ sniffed. "I notice some don't agree with me," he said. "That Urho, for instance. Probably ought to have his eyes examined."

" 'Good, great and joyous, beautiful and free; This is alone Life, Joy, Empire and Victory!' " I hollered spitefully.

"You are getting worse, not better. You must've made that up yourself. Sounds too terrible to belong to anybody else."

"It's beautiful and it was written by Shelley."

"Smelly Shelley. Keep your danged fool poetry to yourself." The way he said the word it came out *potry*. He skipped off down the road ahead of me, leaving me to trundle the cart all the way back to House Place by myself.

"Sticks and stones," I said. "Just you remember, I'm going to be famous someday."

"Might as well be," he hollered back. "Ain't no sensible man going to look at you after you open your mouth with all that weird talk."

Now hadn't a variety of adjectives been applied to me as I strolled through life? Old. Wise. Pitiful. Weird. The last by my own brother, who surely ought to've known better. Besides which, it was not true that no man would ever love me. I knew perfectly well that one already did. That, however, was no one's business but my own. I trundled faster toward House Place and studied the sky as I did so: I had just enough time to deliver the chips and run to the school to pick up a book Miss Pratt had left for me before she went on her vacation to San Francisco.

I had only got part way to school, however, before the snow started to fall. But the weather leaned to the warm side for November and the large white flakes melted almost as soon as they hit the sere prairie grass. I decided to keep going rather than turn back. If, by chance, the weather took a serious turn for the worse I would stay at the school until the storm had passed. I knew there was wood stored out back; maybe Miss Pratt had even left some tea in a tin at her desk.

"This book is really too old for you, Willie," she had admitted. "But do with it what you can. It might not make sense to you now, but later on you will remember some of what you read." *The Rise and Fall of the Roman Empire.* The only thing I knew about Rome was that it was where John Keats lay sleeping under his blanket of daisies. It was enough to lure me on.

I ran nearly the whole last mile, partly afraid of being caught in the snow, partly eager to see just how hard the book was going to be. When I got within a few yards of the school I was amazed to find footprints going ahead of me, straight up to the door, which was closed. Maybe it was Miss Pratt, who had decided not to lend me the book after all. . . .

But who should stand in the middle of the room, flushed and pale-eyed, but Urho Kiiskaala. "What in tarnation are you doing here?" I said. I regretted the peevishness of my voice as soon as the words were out.

"I have walked from Fargo today," he said. "I was tired. When I got to the school, I thought it would be fine to rest awhile before going on. But I will leave quickly. I did not know I should not have come in."

"Shoo," I said. "I only came myself to fetch home a book Miss Pratt promised to leave for me." I glanced at the desk; it was there, just as she had promised it would be. "I'll make a fire and put on some tea, providing Miss Pratt has any in her desk. We can both rest a minute before setting out for home." He watched, somewhat amazed, as I seized hold of the situation. I dashed outside, gathered prairie hay for tinder, and fetched wood from the end of the schoolhouse. I built a fire, skipped out for water from the rain barrel, skimmed the ice off it, put a kettle on to boil for tea.

It wasn't many minutes before he was warming his hands around a mug, the skin over his knuckles stretched red and raw. "It is nice here," he said. "Snug and warm. Someday I too will have such a snug, warm place of my own." He strained his tea through his teeth and seemed to reflect on matters of considerable consequence.

"I am eighteen years old now. Old enough to file a land claim. That is why I traveled to Fargo. My land will adjoin my father's. Between us we have nearly eight hundred acres in the family. Someday I will get citizenship papers, too. I will really be an American, then. But first you will have to teach me all about your Constitution and the names of all your presidents."

We stood side by side in front of the black stove. "No trouble," I assured him. His eyes glowed into mine. As eyes went they were nice ones, fringed with their little golden brushes, but persisted in bending on me a glance I was not prepared to accept. Yet.

"My father was eighteen when he was married," Urho informed me.

"That a fact?" I remarked crisply and stirred the fire in my most businesslike manner.

"Wil-leeee. . . ." Long pause. "Wil-leeee, do you think . . . you will get married someday?"

Tarnation. *"Married?"* I howled. "I'm not even fifteen years old yet. Won't be for another five months. It is much too early to even think of such a thing."

"My sister Lenna, the one we left behind in Finland, she was fifteen when she married Jalmar. She has a baby now. She was afraid she might be an old maid."

"Lordy. That is certainly not one of the concerns that keeps me awake at night. Besides, I have got to finish school."

"Why?"

Now, if he had to ask, how was I going to explain it to him? I would simply outline for him the map I had drawn of my life. "I am going to be a writer," I said. "Even people in Memphis are going to read my books someday. Maybe Mobile, too."

"You can write to my sister Lenna," he beamed, pleased as a child by the thought. His pale eyes twinkled like two stars close to my own. I felt myself getting warm and so stepped back a pace from the fire. "I have already told her about you, Willie," he said, following me. "I have told her that you are as *kaunis* as she is."

"*Kaunis*. Now what's that supposed to mean?"

"It means beautiful."

"Tsk, tsk, poor thing. If the Lord didn't do any better by her than he did by me, she's in serious trouble."

"You work very hard, too," he added, admiring my fire, my pot of boiling water. "That is good in a woman."

"Well," I agreed modestly, "now you are talking some sense." I peered out the window. The wind had come up something fierce and I couldn't see four feet beyond the pane for the heavy white curtain that had been drawn across it. "I certainly hope we don't have to camp here all night."

"It is better than freezing in the storm."

"Belle and Mr. B. are going to have the fan-tods, wondering where I am," I fussed.

"The fan-tods?"

"Jitters. I didn't tell them where I was headed. Only TJ."

"In Finland we would not think to go off on a winter's day without telling exactly where we were going. It is a country that teaches you respect for winter. Perhaps I am more wary of such weather than you are."

"Doubtless. After all, I hardly knew what snow looked like, coming from Tennessee."

"Ten-a-see. It sounds soft and pretty."

"It was. Green, too. We had lots of chinaberry trees—my favorite kind. It was to me what Finland was to you."

"How so?"

"Home. The place I was exiled out of. Not by my own choice. A place I'd like to go back to some day."

"I don't want to go back to Finland. No. There are more opportunities here." Again, his eyes glowed.

"That's your opinion, my friend."

"Am I? Your friend?"

"Of course. Ain't I already spent two months teaching you your letters and all? Didn't I agree to help you with the Constitution? I wouldn't waste my time on just any old person." *And that's all I aim for you to be, too,* I might've added, but didn't. *Just a friend.*

By the time the snow had stopped falling, it was too dark to see a blamed thing. There was nothing for us to do but bank the fire and wait until morning. I headed for the door to fetch a few more sticks of wood.

"Wil-leeee, let me do it," Urho reprimanded me gently. "Let me get the wood."

I stood aside, held the door, and felt a fool, as he did so. The room remained far from overheated so we pulled two desks close to the stove. I folded my arms across the top of mine and laid my head down.

"Your filly—she is like the snow," Urho's sleepy voice came to me. "So clean. So white."

"That's why I call her the Snowbird."

"The Snowbird. That is nice. In Finn we would say *Lumi Lintu.*"

"That's pretty, too: *Lumi Lintu.* Like poetry."

"And Wil-leee?" My name on his lips was soft as a caress in the darkness.

"What?"

"Truly, you are *kaunis*."

"Hush," I said.

Belle and Mr. B. did indeed have a bad case of the fan-tods. When I walked into the house the next morning, the storm having passed by in the night and having left the prairie drenched in thin November sunshine, their relief was of a rambunctious kind.

"Lord, Lord, Willie! We thought we'd find you froze stiff come springtime," Belle cried. "TJ finally told us where you'd gone but we had no way of knowing if you'd got there before the storm got really bad. People have been killed out here for better reasons than running off to fetch some silly book."

"It seemed like a good enough one to me," I said airily.

"What's the name of it, if it's so precious?"

"The Rise and Fall of the Roman Empire."

"Can't see it'd ever make much difference why the empire went up or came down if you've been turned into an icicle."

"Belle," I said, "I reckon it sort of means to me what a piece of stained glass means to you."

She cut me a bright green glance at those impudent words, but rather than scold, she clapped me warmly against her. "I know, Willie, I know. Our dreams might be different, yours and mine, but under the skin we are alike as two peas." Well. I was not sure I agreed with her, but I knew the atmosphere at House Place surely would not be improved if I confessed I had not spent the night alone at the school.

Belle released me after a noisy buss on the cheek and twirled me around to face the back kitchen wall. "Actually, Willie, I was only afraid that we might not get you thawed out enough to appreciate our gorgeous posters!" For there they were, already tacked up: huge, filled with gaudy color, scenes from Morocco, Port-au-Prince, and Paris. "Ain't they grand, Willie?"

Belle demanded. "Why, it's almost like being right there!"

"Yes, ma'am," I agreed, and read aloud from the poster of Port-au-Prince: " 'Capital, chief port, and commercial center of the West Indian republic of Haiti, situated on a magnificent bay at the apex of the Gulf of Gonâve, built by the French in 1749. The city boasts of the finest thoroughbred horses in the world and has regular shipboard connections with New York and ports in the Caribbean.' "

"We'll all go there someday," Belle promised, "after one of those years when we sell a trillion tons of wheat, or maybe by that time we'll be into the beef cattle business and will be known as the Beef Barons of the Dakota Territory!"

I raised a brow but she would not be deterred: "Oh, I know it'll happen, all right." She winked sassily. "I just know it will."

It was afternoon before I could slip away to the barn to be alone with the Snowbird. There may have been human ears into which I might've poured my dilemmas, but I always felt more comfortable confiding in her. The dense winter coat beneath my fingers was like a blanket, thick and soft and silver, and I told her of my consternation concerning a certain male person.

"He's got ideas too old for the likes of me," I said, brushing her silver mane until it rippled like a waterfall. "But while he might be wrongheaded as a goose on some points, he's sure right about one thing: says I'm a hard worker. As for that *kaunis* business—well, I don't believe it any more'n he does."

"Sounds like your love life is getting awful complicated," came a voice from the darkness. Might've known it. July Chemeliewski had the biggest ears in the Territory. Never missed a lick.

"With two million acres out here," I groused, "anybody'd think I could find someplace to speak a few private thoughts."

"Keep the tail on the hide, sis. No need to take offense."

"Ain't you a card though?"

"Speaking of cards," he said, "you want to play a hand or two of blackjack when you're through fussing with the Bird? It's a decent enough way to while away a winter afternoon."

"Why not?" I sighed. Our quarrels, though frequent, were short and pointed in nature. Through the open door of his cubbyhole I saw him set up the applebox chair for me, haul out the busted wagon seat for a table. His tiny stove glowered cheerfully in the corner. When I had finished with the Bird, I picked up my five cards, all bad ones, which I nevertheless studied and held close to my nose.

"I didn't really aim to insult you, sis," he said, taking my silence for a set of hurt feelings.

"You mean for giving me five lousy cards?"

"For telling you to keep the tail on the hide."

"I've heard worse advice. Not that I asked for any, of course."

"Most females don't, I've noticed. Not to mention any names."

"You are always criticizing Belle," I said, leaping to conclusions.

"Sometimes I think it'd been a kindness on her part to've left your uncle where he was, in New York, playing his piano."

"It was Boston. And the instrument happened to be a violin. Hit me with another card."

"Whatever." He threw down another card.

"Besides, I thought it was him who brung her out here, not the other way around."

"By no means, sis. She got a bee in her bonnet, that lady did, probably after reading one of them Chicago and Northwestern advertisements. "The U.S. government offers two million farms to two million families who will occupy and improve them . . . these lands lie between the forty-fourth degree and the forty-eighth degree of latitude, and between the Minnesota and the Missouri rivers. In this belt is thirty millions of acres. . . .' I seen them posters myself. But your auntie don't have the heart for homesteading, for the grinding-down sort of effort it takes to make it out here. Travel posters and parties, that's more her style."

"Blackjack," I said, and flung down my hand. I had played to win while he had been nattering on. I fixed him with a narrow stare. "I think you love her," I said.

He didn't have the good sense to act surprised. "Love her? Why, sholey. Just like you do. Like TJ does. Like we all do. How can we help it? And not just on account of she's pretty as a peeled onion. Only, you know how much difference it's going to make, whether we love her or not?"

"How much?"

"Stick your finger in a pail of water, sis, and see what sort of a hole you leave behind. Whether we love her or not, in the long run that's how much difference it will make."

July's words might've left a deep impression except something else left a deeper one: Miss Pratt never came back from San Francisco. Instead, she sent me a letter. "I am sorry, Willie, but my friend and I have decided to stay here. Please forgive me and try to understand I didn't plan it that way. Don't let anyone steal your dreams and please keep the book I gave you."

But I was so angry that it was a long, long time before I could even open it. Like Belle said, did it really matter why the empire went up or came down?

13

As Christmas came near Belle baked herself into a regular fit. Nowhere, at any time, not even when we stayed those three months at Mr. Rich's, had we seen provender stored up in such amounts. Not that we could afford it. Our wheat had gotten hailed out that spring, the twenty sheep that Mr. B. tried to run ate jimsonweed and died, every darned dumb one of them, and the brown cow dropped a stillborn calf. Our poverty was something Belle took slight account of, however.

She made date cakes and cookies dipped in sugar. She tried her hand at homemade mints and cranked them out by the dozens in yellow, pink, and green. TJ and I pulled taffy until our arms like to fell off. Hard-boiled eggs, pickled in spices and floating in beet juice, hovered in a glass jar like pale oval moons. July purchased a gift for the family: a huge salted ham that he fetched home from Red River.

"But the rest of you, meaning mostly you two children, will make homemade presents this year. Nothing that costs money, hear? Lord knows I've spent enough for all of us already," said Belle.

She wrote names on slips of paper in her spidery script, folded each piece four times, and shook them in her lavender traveling hat. Blindfolded and thrilled, TJ and I chose ours. I opened mine slowly; what in the world could I invent for the likes of a person like July?

But the name on my paper contained five letters, not four: *Belle*.

TJ, who'd drawn Mr. B.'s name, collapsed in a regular hizzy-fit. "I don't know how to make anything, Willie! I suppose you already got some grand notion up your sleeve for Belle. That's the only thing you're really good at—thinking up stuff."

"Thanks a lot."

"You going to help me make something for Mr. B.? I suppose you will make a poem for Belle." He rearranged the four letters of the word so they came out *pome*.

"What I'm making for her is a secret. You'll find out when we open our presents. But a poem is a good idea—and I'll help you write one for Mr. B." He made a face, but how many other choices did he have? It was a poem or an empty hand; he accepted my offer.

The very day Belle announced our gift-giving, I began to save all the combings I got from the Snowbird's mane. Long, silvery strands they were, silken yet possessed of a magical vitality that amazed me. I combed them straight and stashed them inside my pillow case until I had collected a goodly lot of them. When the supply seemed adequate, I asked July to help me make the ring.

"Ring? Tarnation. Made out of horsehair, you say?"

"Yep. Now hang on to these three strands while I plait them together," I said.

"Where'd you learn such arts?"

"Back in Tennessee. Me and Beth Ellen used to make wishing rings out of one another's hair. She wore a ring of my hair, I wore one of hers. That's when I had hair, of course."

"Speaking of that, whatever happened to yours?"

"Rat chewed it all off one night. It was a terrible surprise to everyone."

"I'll bet it was." He didn't believe me and I didn't expect him to."

"Do they work? Wishing rings, I mean."

"Now that you mention it, no. Maybe it was because

those rings were made out of the hair of a person. And Beth Ellen never really wanted to do me a good turn anyhow. But this ring'll be different. Made out of the silver hair of a silver horse, woven when the moon is full."

"Watch those figments, sis. They're leaking out again. Good thing they don't bite like lice."

I plaited three hairs at a time, a trick because they were so fine and seemed to dance in my fingers as if bewitched. When I had woven three strands three separate times, I wove those three together to form an even larger braid, the whole of which was still no larger than the core of a lead pencil. I repeated the process two more times, so that I now had three lead-pencil-sized strands. These, then, were braided into a single strand and pressed flat with my fingers so that I had a thin band of what looked to be real silver. I used my own third finger to measure the ring size and wove the strands back upon each other as in French braiding or rope splicing. I slipped my creation onto my own finger and admired it.

"Now ain't you clever as a speckled pup sleeping in the shade," July marveled. "If I didn't know better I'd say you'd make a feller a pretty fair mate someday."

"You sure ought to know better," I said.

Then I gave assistance to TJ in the construction of his poem.

> Merry Christmas to you, Mr. B.:
> Without your kind heart, where would I be?
> Lonely orphan but loyal and true—
> I sure am glad to be here with you.

"You sure he's going to like that?" TJ asked. He liked it himself: a tear of pleased grief hovered in the tail of his eye.

"He'd better," I said, "for it's the best I got in me at the moment."

On Christmas Day, Belle insisted that we could not eat until it got dark, which it did early since there was a storm coming on. Then, rather than light the kerosene lamp, she dove headfirst into her magical trunk from whence so many good things came, rummaged about, and surfaced with a green candle in one hand and a red one in the other.

"I knew I was saving these for some good reason," she told us. She lit them one at a time and when each dripped vigorously, let the wax fall into a saucer, making a puddle. Quickly, before it hardened, she stuck each candle into the warm pool of its own wax and held it there until it would stand upright by itself.

We sat ourselves, feeling special and self-conscious. "July," Mr. B. asked, "would you care to say grace for us?"

July hesitated only a moment. "Bless these vittles and us that eats 'em," he prayed.

"Amen," said Mr. B., to make it official, and we dove to the task. House Place became a snowbound ark and we shoveled food into our mouths with the mania of shipwrecked folk while the storm raged outside. When we were finished, when the last crumb of mince pie smothered in rum sauce had been consumed, we traded gifts.

I held my breath as Belle began to peel back the folds of the scrap of periwinkle blue fabric from Mama's old dress in which I had wrapped the wishing ring. For a long time she stared at the ring, snuggled in its periwinkle nest. She picked it up at last and slid it onto her finger.

"Ah, Willie—a wishing ring!"

"How'd you know what it was?" I was astonished.

Her eyes were sly and pleased. "Didn't I tell you we were not so different, you and me? I used to make them out of my sister's hair."

"Sister! I didn't know you had a sister! What was her name? Was her hair as red as yours?"

"It was a long time ago," she said, turning my questions away. "And now I have something for all of you to share," she went on. She picked up a small package and placed it on her knees.

"It don't look big enough for *all* of us," TJ speculated. "Unless it's candy and extra sweet." I knew that is what he hoped.

"Oh, this will be quite large enough to share," Belle assured him. "This is the sort of present that grows on you, you might say. It's not nearly as small as it looks. Here, Willie, you open it and show it to everyone."

I pulled away the tissue, which in the candle glow took on the color of ripe peaches. Something gleamed beneath the tissue and when the last scrap had been lifted away, I saw a garment that might have been made by elves or fairies. It was yellow, Belle's favorite color, frothy with lace and ribbons, but so tiny it could only have fit a doll or a baby.

Or a baby.

"Next summer," Belle said, "we will have someone here to wear this dress. And because this is the merriest Christmas I have ever had, when in spite of everything—the hail and the silly sheep—our luck seems to be changing, and because I know in my bones that this baby will be a girl, I want to name her after Willie and me and the season itself. We'll call her Merribelle Willanna Bannerman. She'll be healthy and happy, all apricots and roses, and will bind us up like a real true family."

TJ laced his fingers over his heart. "And I won't be the youngest person around here anymore," he said. July studiously inspected his knuckles, as if noticing for the first time their peculiar charcoal color. Mr. B.'s forehead, worry written all across it, was flushed in the candleglow.

"I know it will be different this time, Belle," he said. "Just you wait and see. It will be different this time around."

That night, since the storm refused to abate, July slept in House Place on a quilt folded up in front of Herschvogel. To hear the storm rage beyond the attic ceiling, to look down the trapdoor opening to see July curled before the Grimm brothers' talking stove, to hear Belle and Mr. B. stir in their brass boat, gave me a stitched-together feeling. *It will be different this time around,* Mr. B. had said. What had happened, in those days before TJ and I ever arrived in the Territory?

But I would not trouble myself over it, I decided. When Merribelle arrived, it would be just like Belle predicted: we would be a real true family.

14

"Willie? You ever think about home anymore?"

"Home?" My tone was blank. I could not imagine for a minute what he was talking about. "You mean Tennessee? Why no, TJ, not hardly at all. House Place is home now. Ain't you used to it yet?"

"Oh, sure," he answered, a shade too quickly. "Except once in a while I like to think about that other one. Tennessee. You know something, Willie? It's a pretty name to say. *Tennessee*." His voice was filled with wishes.

It was only in the quietest times that I ever thought about it, mainly in the floaty time just before sleep. Then I would see again the confabulation of Wash McDermott's whiskers, would wonder if anyone had planted white carnations beside the pink marble goneness of William and Anna Bannerman. Accident, Mr. Rich had tried to impress on me. Accident, my elbow. I knew what I knew.

I, for one, had no time for accidents. None would ever happen to me if I could help it. So when I traveled to meet Urho Kiiskaala that morning at our abandoned schoolhouse—no teacher having been found to take Miss Pratt's place—I led the Snowbird at my side. Would I bother to explain her presence to him? No; either he would not understand or he would be insulted. But she would give us something to talk about besides ourselves; most particularly I did not want to talk about ourselves. After all, he knew (for I'd told him myself) that I'd had my fifteenth birthday.

Urho was sitting cross-legged in the middle of the road as I came down its length. He seemed pleased that I had brought the Bird with me. "When will you be able to ride her?" he wanted to know. Already it was working: he was talking about her, not me.

"Oh, Lordy, not for a long time yet. She's only twenty months old; that's about eleven or twelve years old for a person. July says I can sit on her back once in awhile, ride her around the corral for a few minutes now and then. But nothing more. That much won't hurt, he says, considering I don't weigh much more than a sack of spuds."

Like a shadow cast over the prairie by wind-driven clouds, an elfish grin crossed Urho's face. "I don't believe it," he said. "Here, let me see for myself." So saying, he jumped up, grabbed me around my middle, and hoisted me clean off the ground. My feet dangled in the air. I squealed like any fool female.

"Hey!" I objected, toes grazing the grasstops. "You're going to scare the Snowbird."

"You are the one who's scaring her. It's you who sounds like a milk pail full of rocks."

He let me down but didn't loosen his hold around my waist. I glanced down at the hands clasped firmly around my midsection. His wrists were braceleted with wiry hairs the color of oat straw; his knuckles were enlarged and scarred from cold weather and hard work. But why did I feel like I moved in a dream or that my arms and legs would not obey sensible commands? He held me fast and directed my glance across the prairie that stretched before us.

"I sowed my hundred and sixty acres all in wheat this spring, Wil-leee. In Finland I could never have done so much so quickly. My father says a hardworking man can make a fortune in this country and I believe him," he dreamed.

"You got lots of company," I said. "Pretty soon there won't be any room left for us poor people." Still he kept his arms fastened around my body. Their presence caused my heart to beat too fast and encouraged a peculiar feeling in my stomach. Then he released me, turned me like a top, and before I could stop the fool, planted a kiss right on my mouth. His lips were firm and full and very warm. I hung onto him for dear life and kissed him right back—a fact that might've surprised him some, but terrified the wits right out of me.

I jumped away like I'd been stung on the nose by a bee. "If this is the way you're going to act I'm going to have to stop helping you with the presidents and the Constitution," I threatened.

"I'm nearly a grown man, Wil-leee," he hollered right back, "and my father says it's time for me to settle down. Says it's easier to run a place with a wife. You work hard and that is good in a woman. You'd be a good wife." As dreams go, his were clearly different than mine.

"No, I wouldn't. It ain't my style."

"If we got married you could bring your horse with you," he said. The ultimate enticement, he hoped. "Your uncle would make you a present of the *Lumi Lintu* for your wedding."

"Presents, pheasants," I hollered. Then I tried on him the patient tone you use for someone who doesn't have a full set of dishes. "Urho, I want to go to school. Somehow, sometime. Even though she ran off, I want to have what Miss Pratt had. An education. I don't think I want to get married for a long time."

"Everyone wants to get married. Sooner or later."

"For me, it'll most likely be later." We stood side by side, surveying the immensity of the red prairie. "Whyn't you court Kaia Gunderson?" I said. "She wants to get married."

"Did she tell you that?"

"She didn't have to. I can tell. Women know about that sort of thing."

"Wil-leee, you are a mystery."

"How so?"

"You claim women know that sort of thing. Only there's something in you that doesn't want to be a woman."

"That ain't true," I said. Or was it? Was I some sort

of freak? Would I end up in a circus, the Famous Half-Girl, Half-Boy from the Prairie? Was that what wanting to be a writer was going to mean? "I don't aim to be baking sixteen loaves of bread and six different sorts of pie every morning to feed a thrashing crew, like Mrs. Gunderson," I said. "And babies might be fine, but I don't need a sea of 'em pushing on my knees like water on a dike by the time I'm twenty-three." Besides, I didn't have TJ all raised up yet.

"You are like your aunt."

"Like my *aunt?*" I echoed, stunned. "You must've taken leave of your senses. I am *not* like my aunt! Besides, she *is* married and soon to have a baby, which makes her just like any other homesteader's wife."

He leaned across the Snowbird's neck and stared into the distance. Blood fluttered under the skin at his temple like a trapped butterfly. "I'll do it, then," he said.

"Do what?"

"Court Kaia Gunderson." He eyed me through oat-straw lashes to see if I was jealous.

"That's all right by me," I said, more generous than I felt. "It won't matter between you and me. We can still be friends."

"I don't want a friend. I want something more."

Moments ago his arms had been around my waist. I could still feel his mouth on mine, warm and firm and full. Tomorrow night those lips might be pressed just as firmly to Kaia's. Probably she would not holler and give him a lecture, either. "Go ahead," I urged. "But you know, in a way, I do . . . sort of . . . almost . . . love you."

"Enough to get married? Someday?"

What if he was the only one ever to ask? Would I go through life alone forever? But I couldn't say the word: *no*. All I could do was shake my head.

He raised his arms from the Snowbird's back. A few silver hairs clung to the darkness of his wool shirt. He walked away from me down the road and did not look back. His gait was determined, his arms swung lightly at his sides with the bound-up motion of a person who has done hard labor all his days. A suspicious burning tingled under the bridge of my nose. I permitted myself two anemic little sniffles.

You got asked once, Willie Bannerman, I told myself. *Maybe that will have to do.* I'd just have to take my chances.

Now I will admit this: Urho Kiiskaala was a boy— pardon me, a man—of his word. In two days the glow on Kaia's face told me all I needed to know. Lempii was puzzled by the whole thing. "I thought he liked you, Wil-leeee."

"He does. Did. And I like him. Only it was not the kind of liking that heads for the altar."

"Kaia surely believes that's where it's going to lead her."

"Great," I said. "Nobody could be happier for 'em than me."

Kaia was, in truth, in cat heaven. To me, she had never seemed as pretty as Lempii. Now, basking in the determined glow of Urho's pale eyes, she positively bloomed. And now that he liked her, Kaia was free to like me better. It was she who told me, gently, as if the news would permanently unhinge me, "Wil-leee, we are going to get married."

"Good," I declared. "You'll be happy, no doubt about it. It's what you want. Him, too."

"You aren't . . . mad at me?"

Did she think she'd won him away from me? I'd given him to her, that's what—over the back of a silver horse, so to speak. I would like to have told her so. Instead, I said, "Lordy, no. Not a whit. No skin off this old nose."

"I was afraid you would be . . . jealous."

"Not a pea particle," I assured her briskly. And walking home that night, skipping rocks down the dusty road with TJ, I realized I was not. Over tea and potato dumplings and some of Belle's fresh bread, I dropped the news of the approaching nuptials. Mouths opened. Forks dropped. July's blackberry peepers glowed with smug self-satisfaction.

"Finally gave in, huh, sis?"

"Oh, he ain't marrying me," I said.

"Ummmm. Somehow that does not seem to cause you any particular pain or grief."

"Nope. He's marrying Kaia. They want the same things."

"Meaning?"

"Meaning they got acres on the brain. Want a passel of kids to help with chores. Want to take up a life just like their mamas and papas."

"I don't understand you, sis."

"What's to understand?" I groused. "And if you think it's such a great and grand institution, how come you ain't tried it on for size yourself?"

"Aw, no gal would have a feller with a mug like this one."

"Women don't marry mugs, July," Belle put in. "They marry men. Maybe you're just as good as any."

"Anyhow, I aim to be a writer. Maybe a poet, too," I said. " 'Thou unravished bride of quietness, Thou foster child of silence and slow time . . .' "

"I reckon you can count on going unravished a lifetime with words like that hanging on the end of your tongue," July predicted.

I skipped to the door with a lightness I did not entirely feel. "Sticks and stones," I hollered over my shoulder.

"You been called by a boy's name too long, sis," he called after me. He cut me to the bone with that one. He was right: no longer was I a scrawny, putty-eyed person hunkered in the leaves on Mrs. Wilson's hillside. I was fifteen. But still a stranger in my own skin.

That night, when I was sure everyone else was asleep, I lifted myself down the ladder from the loft. It was June and warm and Mr. B. had left the door of House Place standing wide open. I stepped outside. A quarter moon slid like a wedge of lemon pie across the night sky. July always slept like he'd been poleaxed so I did not worry overly much about rousing him or having him accost me with a pitchfork, mistaking me for a chicken thief, or worse, a horsethief.

There have not been many times in my life when I

deliberately did a thing I knew to be wrong. That night was one of them. I took the bridle down from its peg on the barn wall, slid the bit into the Snowbird's mouth. She accepted it easily, as she always did. I drew her close to the corral fence, climbed the bars on the opposite side, eased across the topmost one, and lowered myself onto her back.

"Easy, girl," I whispered into that laid-back silver ear. "It's just old Willie. Old girl-with-a-boy's-name Willie. No need for you to take exception to me now."

She stiffened under me, her muscles gathered together like springs. A long shudder passed through her frame. I remembered how long it'd taken to get her accustomed to the halter and to the lead rope. Now I imagined I heard her moan: *Freedom, gone! Taken away by this skinny female who won't hold with things most females hold with!*

"It's only that I can't dream someone else's dream," I tried to explain. "What's right for Belle or Kaia or Beth Ellen ain't necessarily right for me." I waited for her to uncoil herself and send me headlong into the dirt where she figured I belonged. But slowly, slowly, as July had predicted, the tension eased out of her frame. She turned her head, nuzzled my bare toes with her soft, damp nose.

I placed my two hands across her neck. Had the horse Pauline Cushman rode been white? Did the banner men, back there in the olden golden days of England, ride steeds of silver? I guided her around the corral in the faint moonlight, sidled her up to the latch on the gate and let it drop. The gate swung open of its own weight. We stepped out onto the moon-tarnished prairie, no horse and rider, but single creature, molded one to the other.

The wind stirred the tall prairie hay against our knees. It lifted the Snowbird's silver mane and brushed it against my cheek. I passed my calves against her silver ribs and she rose, serene and free, toward the low ridge along the Red River where once I'd been sure I'd seen three Sioux braves waiting. We were lifted, no more substantial than milkweed down, toward the

ridge, and it was not until later, when I lay on my half
of our pallet in the attic, that I realized I could not
bring to mind the sound of her hoofbeats against the
earth.

On the crest of that shallow ridge we looked back:
House Place caught the gleam of moon silver on its tin
eaves. Then from far, far away I heard another horse
whinny. It was a thin, imperious cry that froze the
Snowbird in her tracks. She turned her silver face to
the west, ears pricked sharply forward.

Was it a horse from one of the Sioux herds? Had
one of Kiiskaalas' horses gotten loose and was it wan-
ering around, alone, on the moonlit prairie? Or was it
by chance the silver stallion who'd gotten Fanny with
foal? "Let's go back," I whispered, feeling a cool finger
pressed against the nape of my neck. "We shouldn't be
out here anyhow."

As we turned down the slope of the hill I spied
something gleaming in the grass, long and flat and silver. I halted the Snowbird, slid from her back, and
knelt in the grass. It was a wood slab, worn smooth by
wind and rain and snow. I tilted it up so that I could
read its legend aloud to the stars:

JOHN MICHAEL BANNERMAN

BORN JUNE 5, 1883

DIED JUNE 10, 1883

It is good for your wife to have this niece, Mrs.
Gunderson had said. *Won't take the place of the boy,
but it will help.* I slipped the wood marker back into its
niche in the prairie turf. In five days of the same year
Mama and Papa had been burned up, John Michael
Bannerman had been born, lived, and passed into eter-
nity. Not much of a life—for him or those who'd
waited for his coming.

I gave a jump; the Snowbird dipped a bit to ease me
on again, and we flew back to House Place. In the corral, I slipped from her silky back, took the bridle off,

hung it on its peg in the barn. I took her silver face in my hands and kissed the whorled silver star between her wide, dark eyes. *"Lumi Lintu,"* I whispered. "Little white bird of the snows." But instead of listening to me, she pressed her head over the top bar of the corral, yearning to hear again that long, thin mysterious call to freedom.

It was the next morning, two hours after July and Mr. B. set out to harvest our forty acres of oats that lay near the edge of the Gunderson place, that TJ cried out to me, "Willie! Willie! Come quick! Something's happened to Belle."

15

I would travel twice around the world, walk cobbled streets far from the Territory, eat tangerines beside blue seas, visit Tipton, where I would discover Beth Ellen wasn't as grand as I'd remembered her to be, and have babies of my own before TJ's shrill cry would stop ringing in my ears:

"Something's happened to Belle. . . ."

I dropped the dish towel and flew into the yard, looking first one way and then another. She was spread-eagled on the ground, the sacrificial victim of some pyramid-climbing race. The sun scalded down on her and the whole world was milky-white from heat. A hard, hot wind blew up from the south and sucked moisture from my cheeks, arms, hair roots.

I ran to where she lay. "What happened?" I asked. My voice was small and thin. My body cast a narrow shadow on the ground, scarcely covering the face that was a small, pale oval against the earth. "What happened?" I whispered again.

"I fell," came her reply. Her voice was clear and calm and not afraid. "I don't know exactly how it happened, Willie. Twisted my ankle, maybe. Came down like a sack of barley. Then I felt it; like a rip or a tear." She reached down and cupped her belly between her hands.

"What should I do?"

"Help me get into the house. Out of this sun, out of this heat. I'll just lay down a spell. Maybe it's nothing. Might not mean a thing."

She reached a lean, white arm around my neck. With TJ on the other side I managed to pull her to her feet. But once up she couldn't stand, so we half-carried, half-dragged her into the house. Inside, it was blessedly cool and dark. We hauled her toward the brass bed.

"Towels, Willie, towels," she said. "Put some towels on the bed."

I grabbed a handful quick off the string on the wall and spread them over the quilts. She fell onto them and we straightened her haunches around and hoisted her feet up. I arranged pillows under her knees. TJ ran to the corner to fetch a dipperful of water that I held to her lips.

She drank slowly and her eyes never left mine. Her face was ghastly pale, her eyes full of knowing. "Merribelle's coming before her time, Willie," she said. "She ought not to be in such a rush, but I suspect she'll be here before night comes."

I took Belle's hand in mine. It was cool and her fingers were brittle white twigs in my brown ones. I wetted a rag in the dipper TJ held for me and dampened her forehead.

"Should I be doing anything special to get ready, Belle?" *How am I going to deliver a baby into this world?* I wondered, remembering how reluctant the Snowbird had been to be born, how we had to pry her into the light of day. Surely, surely, Mr. B. and July would soon be home.

"You'd better run to fetch Mrs. Gunderson, Willie. She'll know what to do. She's birthed a lot of babies in her day, her own and others. Maybe if I'd someone like her with the boy it would've ended differently. You got to go fetch her, Willie."

"It's more'n fifteen miles to the Gunderson place, Belle. It'll take me hours to walk that far. I can't leave you all alone with nobody but TJ to look after you. Mr. B. is bound to be back soon. . . ."

She studied me for a long and awful minute.

"Take the Snowbird, Willie. There isn't much time. It's the only thing you can do." It wasn't fair: only a scant two hours had passed since July and Mr. B. had left the yard with Fanny and the pony—and even Sorry.

I did not want to hear her say it. Not the Snowbird. *No*. She was no more than a child herself. Not even a full two years in age. Would not be a two-year-old until November. Was equivalent to about twelve years of age in human terms. Would a human child less than twelve years old be able to take on a task like what Belle was asking of the Snowbird? *No*. July had warned me many times how careful I must be, that I might ruin her if I was too impatient. *No*.

Belle's brittle fingers moved against mine. "Remember what we said, Willie? When the Snowbird was born? She will bring us good luck, Willie. She will— and bring good luck for Merribelle, too."

I nodded. I fetched more towels and spread them under her. I got fresh water so that TJ would have plenty while I was gone. Then I drew him outside with me before I went across the yard to the barn.

His freckles stood out across the bridge of his nose. His bruised eyes were as wide and dark as they were the morning we left Tennessee. A nerve jumped and danced at his temple.

"You going to be all right, Bubba?"

"Yep, I'll be all right, Willie. Only hurry." I stared down at him as silently as he stared up at me. He clasped his hands prayerfully together, level with his breastbone.

"Keep a damp rag on her forehead," I instructed. "Pat her hands. Talk nice to her. I'll be back with Mrs. Gunderson as quick as I can."

The Snowbird dozed in the cool darkness of the barn. She whickered softly, surprised to see me at such a strange midday hour. I took the bridle down from its peg on the wall and put it on her without looking into her eyes. I knew what she did not know: after this ride, which was coming too soon in her life but which she had to make, nothing would ever be the same for either of us. In ways and manners I could not yet perceive.

I cradled her slim, sweet, silver face close to my body. I rocked her gently from side to side. I did not want to look into her eyes. Then I did: looked long and deep into wide, wet, morning glory eyes that had the power to make me feel the world was good, that all things were possible.

The flesh around her eyes was dark; the delicate hairs that spread in a deep ring about them was dark, too, giving the entire orb a depth to which I cannot now do justice. Shy, mild eyes they were, harboring a patience old as the hills as Andalusia and an unquenchable spirit from a great-great-grandsire who had wandered free and wild in the Florida everglades before he rocketed onto the Western plains.

"I love you," I told her. Words I had never said to a human creature. "No matter what happens today, never forget I love you."

I led her out of the sod barn into the blazing Dakota sunshine. I looked up through slotted eyes. The sky was white, the blue bleached out of it by the terrible hot, dry heat. Waves rose off the iron-hard yard in dancing ribbons. The doorgrass was wilted; weeds drooped from the roof of House Place. I jumped onto the Snowbird's back and turned her west, straight into the sun. She stepped out easily, eager to please. She did not know that fifteen long and terrible miles lay ahead of us.

I did not look back at House Place or search its windows for the melting oval blur that would be TJ's frightened face. No matter what else happened, I would be accountable.

16

"Everything is going to be fine," I said. "Things will work out; they always do. This time, too." I almost believed my own words. After all, weren't they familiar, being the selfsame ones I'd used to comfort TJ that last morning in Tipton?

"But I am not going to do you dirt by riding you the whole way. No, ma'am. I will make it as easy for you as I can and yet try to make as good time as possible."

I jumped from her back after we'd gone but a mile or two. I ran in front of her, holding onto the reins, so that she'd be relieved for a short while of my ninety pounds. I ran beside her until my chest shrieked, until my ears pounded with the roar of blood and my eyes felt as if they would fall out of my head. Sweat ran down my forehead, stung my eyes, dripped off the end of my nose. Still I ran. And ran.

When I climbed on her again I told myself that she was rested. It was a hope I hung onto with something akin to rage. We came to a ditch, half-filled with muddy, stagnant rainwater and unappetizing to look at. But it was wet, so I led the Snowbird into it. I let her drink only a few mouthfuls, then held her back from drinking too much. I bathed her chest and limbs, wetted my handkerchief and drizzled water over her face. She submitted gratefully, eyes half-closed, head lowered to the level of my waist.

I led her out of the ditch and wrung the water out of my skirt. Water squirted out of my shoes, leaving my feet cool and soothed. When I mounted again, the

Snowbird ran like an angel, her wet forelock slapping sharply on my cheek till the wind blew it dry and silky again.

It was one of those Dakota summer afternoons when the sky was like a giant's eye, staring down, never blinking, its gaze harsh and unforgiving. When the sun began its westward descent, it became even hotter; the glare seared our eyes like a curse. No wind stirred the scorched grasstops. There had been days in the past when I had longed for the wind to stop its infernal blowing—now I prayed for a breeze, just a whisper, to cool us. None came.

The Snowbird's gait began to falter. Her breath sounded labored, came in shorter and shorter gasps. Four . . . five . . . six . . . how many miles had we covered? I could only guess, having no way to mark them off. I leaped down from her back again, ran in front of her, ran until I nearly fainted, climbed back on and rode some more, only to repeat it all.

It isn't fair. Three of the worst words in the English language, but they circled round and round in my head, three coon hounds on the trail of the masked bandit. *It isn't fair.* Not fair that Merribelle should have to come before her time. Not fair to ask this journey of the Snowbird. Not fair that I should have to break a pledge. No one will ever harm you, I had told her. I choked to recall the words.

"Haven't you learned a fool thing from life, Willie Bannerman?" I asked. "Didn't Tipton County, Tennessee, teach you what to expect?"

But I always hoped for better. All I could depend on now was that July had been right: that the Snowbird came from a long line of greathearted horses, horses whose ancestors had flown across the deserts of Spain, horses that didn't know how to give up.

A deep, clay-banked arroyo opened up under us, a slash in the earth caused by some primordial upheaval. I led the Snowbird into it. The shade of its steep banks umbrellaed us and I fell down in a grateful heap. The Snowbird stood above me, breath coming in long, slow, wheezing groans. The delicate curve of her silver chest was gray with sweat that looked like greasy soapsuds. She braced herself on her forelegs as though not sure she could remain upright without being so propped up. I counted out slowly, "one . . . two . . . three . . . four . . . five . . ."

All the way to sixty. When we'd had a minute's worth of rest, I led her back out of the arroyo, back into the sun, mounted her, set her into a gallop again. "It's all the time we can spare," I told her, hoping she understood. "Belle said the baby would be here before nightfall. Mrs. Gunderson's got to be there before Merribelle is."

Was it my imagination—or did the words put new energy into those silver limbs? I had thought she was the color of courage; now she proved me right. Even when I tried to slow her, she broke back into a long, mile-eating gallop. To this day, I believe the Snowbird knew what was at stake. Perhaps she remembered, in some dim way, the efforts we'd made to get her born. Perhaps.

Her mane whipped my cheeks, stung my lips. Soon the smoothness disappeared entirely from her gait. It became hard and choppy and rattled my kidneys right up to my shoulder blades. My head ached; I saw double of everything. There were two horizons, one on top of the other. Two suns, paired clouds on the skyline. In back of all those double images was a single one: the sight of Belle, spread-eagled on the ground, lying in the shadow cast by my body.

"It's all for Merribelle," I whispered in a flicked-back ear, "for someone we don't even know yet but who'll be all apricots and roses." The specter of a grave board, silvered by moonlight haunted me: John Michael Bannerman, dead before he'd lived a week. Belle's song came back too: *"And I would leave them all for my handsome, winsome Johnnie. . . ."*

"Hurry, Bird, hurry," I called through sun-swollen lips. "It can't be Belle's luck to have that happen again."

Gundersons' place loomed on the horizon, no bigger than a flyspeck. Degree by degree it grew larger. I could see Kaia and Lempii in the garden, each with a kerchief over her head. It was past the supper hour, for I could see Mr. Gunderson turn the cow out after her milking.

It was Lempii who saw me first. She straightened up from her hoeing and shielded her eyes with one hand. She looked like she'd seen an apparition rise from the dead.

"Wil-leeee!" she cried. "What's happened, Wil-leeee? You look so awful. . . ."

"It's Belle," I cried back. "Her baby's coming early. She wants your ma to come. . . ."

"Ma! Ma!" Lempii hollered. "It's Bannermans' baby. *Ma!*"

Kaia hurried to where I had halted the Snowbird. Her eyes were narrowed and hard. Our battle had happened such a long time ago. She had her Finn now; wasn't she ever going to forget? But I saw it was not anger in her eyes, only pity. I didn't know which I despised most, being hated or being pitied. I decided it was the latter.

"Ohhhhhh, your horse," Kaia said. "What has happened to your wonderful silver horse?" She reached out to stroke the Snowbird's neck, but drew her hand away as if afraid.

I slid off the Snowbird's neck and stepped back so that I could see what Kaia saw. I thought I might get sick.

In a few hours' time, during a ride that ought never have been made, the Snowbird's glory had been committed to a silver memory. As in a dream, I felt the warmth of the ashes of the Tipton County *Tribune* as I searched for a talisman. Saw my hair lying on the polished parquet floor of Mrs. Rich's sewing room. What was wrong with my dreams that all of them got broken?

The Snowbird's head hung out on the end of her thin neck like a pumpkin on a frost-withered vine. Her dark eyes were closed as if she pondered an interior view none of the rest of us could see. Blood trickled slowly from one nostril. Her legs were spavined; her tail, once a valedictory banner, hung thin and scraggly against her loins. Greasy sweat, caked with dirt until it was a thick paste, clung to her once-snowy hide.

"She's windbroke," came a voice at my side. I looked up dully to find Mr. Gunderson standing beside me.

"Poor little *flicka*," he said. "Won't likely ever be the same again. She was too young and too fine-boned for the trip you made. Most likely the kindest thing would be to put a bullet through her brain. Might be the kindest thing."

I stared at the wreck of the Snowbird. My lungs wouldn't fill anymore; my heart wouldn't start beating again. I didn't argue with his verdict. It was too late for tears.

"Ya, Jakey," Mrs. Gunderson boomed to one of her older sons. "Hitch the bays to the wagon, Jakey. We got to fairly fly!" I felt her firm hand on my arm. "Come along, child," she said. "It won't do you any good to moon around here. Won't fix up your horse again. Besides, your aunt will need you at home."

I turned to Lempii. "Would you rub her down?" I asked. "It might . . . help."

"I will give her oats, too." Oats; yes, oats might help, if she could eat them. Lempii said no more and I always liked her for that: she knew there were times when the kindest words went unspoken.

I climbed into the buggy beside Mrs. Gunderson. She flicked her whip over the heads of the bays and we flew back to House Place. "I hope Mr. B. got home," I said. "TJ's there all alone. It will have been hard for him." I was drained, limp, all used up.

"Ya," Mrs. Gunderson said. "Ya, a bad thing."

But the yard was empty when we careened into it as the sun was setting. Mrs. Gunderson threw the reins to me, swept up her bag, and sailed across the yard into the house, skirts flapping like waves in the wake of an ocean liner. She flung the door open without knocking. I walked in behind her to see Belle just where I'd left her hours ago. TJ was still glued to the side of the bed.

I couldn't tell which of them was whiter. At first all

I could see of my brother were two round holes that were his eyes, eyes that materialized, unconnected to a body, out of the gloom of that square, suspenseful room.

"I think she's sleeping," TJ said.

"Was it bad?" I asked.

He didn't answer. Two large tears made a gleaming path down either cheek. I hugged him close. "It's all right now," I said. "Everything will be all right now."

Belle opened her eyes. There was no green left in them. That color had been melted away in the long, hot afternoon. "Mrs. Gunderson? Willie, did you bring Mrs. Gunderson?"

Mrs. Gunderson leaned over the bed and placed a brown hand on Belle's belly. "I'm here, Missus Bannerman. How are your pains coming?"

"They . . . go and come," Belle said. "Not hard ones anymore. Not like this afternoon. I can't understand it. I was sure the baby would be here by now. I am tired . . . so tired."

Mrs. Gunderson turned on TJ and me. "You children hustle yourselves outdoors now," she said. "We got some birthing to do and we don't need any distractions." Almost the same words Belle herself had used on us the day the Snowbird was born.

Outside, the air had begun to cool. Lavender shadows snuggled in every corner of the yard, swathed the barn in tranquil light. I could even imagine a moistness in the air.

"I ain't had nothing to eat since you left, Willie," TJ said. "I never got off that stool beside Belle's bed, Willie. It was awful. She cried and cried. I couldn't make her stop. Nothing I did helped at all."

I squeezed his fingers in mine.

"Willie, she was saying it was going to be just like that other time. What'd she mean, Willie? What other time?"

"There was another baby, TJ. Before we ever got to the Territory. His name was John Michael Bannerman. He died after five days." He might as well know all of it. Some things are better off never being hid at all.

"You won't ever know what it was like this afternoon, Willie," he sniffled.

"That's the way it is sometimes, TJ," I said. He
knew only his own part of the afternoon, not mine.
Nor could I know his part. Our lives, it seemed, ran on
parallel tracks but never converged. "After a while
you'll forget," I told him.

He nodded his head, yes, but could not say the
word. His tears had left platinum tracks on his cheeks.
I stroked his head and looked over my shoulder at
House Place. The lamp made a mellow glow through
the window, but there was no sound.

I looked down the road. "Here they come," I told
TJ, and pointed. Mr. B. and July were inching closer
through the twilight. Then I heard it: a high, thin wail
from the house. A cry more like that of a newborn kit-
ten than a human child. Merribelle was alive! All apricots and roses, come to bind us up like a real true
family. I waited for another cry. None came. I let go of
TJ's hand, flew across the yard, and flung open the
door.

17

"She's a blue, breathless mite," Mrs. Gunderson said. "More's the pity; this country's hard enough on the tough ones. No telling how this tyke will fare."

She placed the baby in the shell of my arms. Blue and breathless, maybe, but her hair branded her the daughter of Belle Bannerman. It was bonny and coppery and curled in spidery tendrils at her temples.

"How is she, Willie?" Belle called to me. "How is my wonderful Merribelle . . .?"

I stared down at the baby. She was so frail and breathless I could not have told at which moment her breath stopped altogether. All I knew was the blue faded magically away. In its place came the whiteness of finest porcelain, the kind made into figures of queens and angels and ballerinas that had decorated the top of Mrs. Rich's piano.

"Belle . . ." I did not have to finish. She rose on one elbow out of her brass boat.

"Don't say it, Willie. Don't tell me. If I don't hear the words, it won't be true." She placed her hands over her ears to block out anything I might say. She lay back in her bed, turned to the wall, and hugged herself with her thin white arms. Mrs. Gunderson reached out and plucked Merribelle from my grasp.

"I will prepare the child," she said quietly.

"No," Belle said. "I want Willie to do it. Willie understands. Let Willie do it." She did not turn her face to me as she spoke.

"Yes, Belle," I said. I did not tell her that I understood, for I wasn't sure I did. But I would do as Belle asked: bathe Merribelle and shroud her in the yellow gown. As I prepared to pour water in a shallow pan, the door opened behind me and I turned, Merribelle cupped in one arm, to face Mr. B. He searched my face for the message he longed to hear. He flicked a glance at Mrs. Gunderson. Without a word, he walked into the yard, took the shovel from its place at the corner of House Place, and went straight to the spot where I'd found John Michael's silvered marker.

In the morning, Mr. B. fashioned another pine slab to mark Merribelle's grave. July burned her name into it with a poker heated redhot in a fire built outside. It read:

MERRIBELLE WILLANNA BANNERMAN
DIED JULY 22, 1885

He didn't even put "Born." To me, it was as though she'd never lived at all.

"Dear Lord," Mr. B. prayed, "we ask you to place Merribelle's hand in the hand of the brother she never knew. Please guard them both until we shall all be joined with them in heaven. Amen."

With his bare hands July began to place dirt on top of the tiny pine box that was Merribelle's coffin. Belle, out of bed against Mr. B.s' wishes, watched impassively. "Belle, it will be all right again," Mr. B. said. "It's been a terrible blow, but we'll survive it, just like we survived all the others."

"You still got me," TJ offered hopefully. "You got Willie, too. She looks a whole lot better now her hair's growed out all the way."

I would have liked for Belle to have cried and shrieked, to have fallen to the ground and rolled around screaming and tearing her hair—anything except what she did. She looked past all of us, past the rim of the prairie, over the edge, to some transparent place where dreams are born.

July went with me to fetch the Snowbird home.

"Don't take it all so hard, sister," he said as we bounced along the rutty road after leaving Gundersons'. "Sure, it looks bad right now. Baby's gone. Snowbird seems busted and done for. But maybe there's a way to set it all right again."

His words ignited something flammable inside me. "Are you crazy?" I snapped. "Explain to me, if you can, how are we going to make another Merribelle? How, if it ain't too much trouble, are we going to put fresh wind back in the Snowbird? How're we going to bring rain for a crop that's been burned to a crisp? You put me in mind of some dumb, danged, no-account backwoods preacher. Believe me, it's too late in the day to preach to *me!*"

July snorted. "Maybe I ain't a preacher, sis, but there's some things I believe in. Like possibles. It's just possible, see, that we can doctor the Snowbird up. Possible someday there'll be another baby Bannerman. One that'll be lusty and healthy and will take us all by storm. It's possible."

"No, it ain't. You been out in the sun too long without a hat to cover your brains."

"And you're the kind gets rusty when it rains." No matter that he had made me a rhyme; no such jollification could change my outlook.

"Look at her," I said. "How're you ever going to fix that up?"

The Snowbird plodded along beside the wagon, oblivious to our words, to the day, to our existence. She put one forehoof in front of the other, without spirit, only doing what was necessary to keep perambulating down the road. Her breastbone gleamed through her dull hide like an ax blade. Her silverness was just a remembrance. Her eye sockets were hollow cups where morning glories would never bloom again.

"We can build up her strength. There are ways."

"Mr. Gunderson said the kindest thing would be to put a bullet through her brain."

"Sholey he is being overly pessimistic, even for a Swede."

"He's a Norwegian."

"Whatever. Not even a Norwegian can make me let go my theory of possibles. But you—why, you go ahead and pull the trigger if you want. Only don't ask me to help you."

My hands hunted for each other in my lap. "What, exactly, did you have in mind by saying we could build up her strength?"

"Well, we'll start out by brewing up a mash for her she just won't be able to resist. We'll pump her so full of vim and vigor she won't be able to do anything 'cept get better. We'll exercise her, too, put warm compresses on those muscles that been frozen by strain and overwork. Before you know it, sis, we'll have coaxed that old Snowbird right back into her skin."

"Even the Sioux wouldn't take her now."

"Don't be so negative."

"How long will it take? To fix her up?"

"Who's keeping time, sis? You got someplace special you got to be any certain day?"

"And you claim it's possible?"

"Yep."

Now I knew July's philosophy of possibles would not bear too close a scrutiny: I, Willie Bannerman, for instance, would never be beautiful. Money and Mr. B. would likely remain strangers to each other. Ladies in lace were not apt to throw themselves, deranged by fits of passion, at the feet of a certain Mr. July Chemeliewski. Certain things in this life are *not* possible. Nevertheless, I had to take a chance.

I hied myself out of bed early the next morning, before TJ had stirred or Belle and Mr. B. crept from their brass boat. But I wasn't early enough to beat July. He was waiting for me—I had known he would be—arms crossed over the top pole of the corral. He aimed a smile somewhere over my left ear.

"I knew it," he said. "I can spot another possibles person a mile away."

"Don't let it go to your head. I was that way a long time before I met up with you." It was peculiar: I could speak to July in a manner I would never dared to have used with Mr. B. Or with Papa either. Some people carry barriers around with them. I did it myself. July surrounded himself with nothing more than a picket-fence smile.

I love you, July Chemeliewski.

I was sorely tempted to say the words right then and there. He would not have been embarrassed. Would have said with a shrug, "Well, yes, you're at that awkward age, all right." As always, when it came to such confessions, my tongue was still.

He measured a cup of oats into a pail, then added half a cup of bran and a handful of cracked wheat from the barrel of chicken feed. He already had collected an egg, which now he cracked into the pail, first separating the yolk from the white. Then came two tablespoons of molasses from a jar in his own quarters, all of which he proceeded to stir until it was thick, like a muffin batter. It smelled good enough to eat and I said so.

"Let's hope the Bird agrees with you," he said.

But she did not. She sniffed at our concoction without interest. Her ribs showed through her dingy coat like strings on a broke-down banjo. Finally, she lipped some of it up, chewed wearily, ate perhaps one third of what July had prepared, then turned away.

"She didn't get more'n half a cup down her gullet," I groaned. "It'll take a month of Sundays for her ever to get better at this rate."

"It's enough for now. It's a start. Now we'll set this stuff in a bucket and put it down in the creek where it won't spoil too fast. We'll try her on it again tonight. If she don't eat it then, we'll start all over with a fresh batch tomorrow."

Later he showed me how to massage her legs. With his sausage-fingered, never-clean hands he rubbed each limb with a soothing downward motion. The Snowbird stood, eyes closed, while he lifted each limb in its turn and rubbed, rubbed. She did not seem to know that we cared. July saw my look, for he said softly, "All things are possible, sis. Including brand-new silver horses and rooms painted pink."

18

To TJ's everlasting distress, I took care of all the cooking. Belle slept away most of every day. When she did not sleep, she lay face to the wall, thin arms folded about herself as though affording herself a comfort she would not allow the rest of us to offer.

Every day, Mr. B. tried to say the right kind of words. "My, you look better today, Belle. Yes, I declare you do! I think you've put on a pound or two. Look almost like your old self again, Belle." The words begged on their knees for her to notice he cared. Only grief, for Belle, was like love: she wrapped herself up in it, wore it like it was made only for her.

But there came an evening in September when, if I could not see that any change had taken place for Belle, at least the Snowbird turned a bend in the road. It came nearly six weeks after July and I started our reconstitution program.

"July, *look!*" I called. "Look at the Snowbird!"

He hurried from his cubbyhole in the barn. He stopped short and by the expression on his face I knew he'd never been as sure as he let on that his philosophy of possibles would work.

"Lordy, don't she look fine!" he agreed.

And she did. She had her head up high, as she used to do when any of us approached the corral. She whinnied—oh, it was not the stronghearted whinny of old, but neither was it that tired and raspy sigh we'd gotten used to.

"Another six weeks and she'll be good as new," July said.

"Now all we got to do is get Belle back on her feet."

He gave me a gentle look. "That might be a bigger order," he allowed.

"I'm going to get her now," I said. "Maybe it'll make her feel better to know the Snowbird's getting a second wind."

I hurried to the house. As ever, Belle lay with her back to me, curved in an S of indifference. "Belle? Get up, Belle—there's something you got to see." She did not stir. "Belle, it's the Snowbird. I think she's better. I think she's on the mend, Belle. . . ."

She half-turned toward me. Her eyes were green, glazed. "Some things have gone too far for mending, Willie. Sometimes there ain't no way in the Lord's world of putting them right again."

Then, strangely, Belle got better without help from any of us. One day she lay there, pale and full of her own pain; the next she rose like a phoenix and was the same old radiant, fox-eyed Belle of other days, full of plots and plans and magic.

"I don't know what ailed me." Her tone was sassy and she seemed to have made up her mind about something. "But whatever it was, it's over now." She tore through the house on a cleaning rampage. "Begone, mouse commas!" she decreed, whisking them from the shelves. Herschvogel was blacked and his chrome was polished. TJ and I cut fresh pages from *The Youth's Companion* and the *Saturday Evening Post*, which Belle pasted over the old ones at the kitchen end of the house. She ripped up her pearl-colored dress and made new curtains for the windows, which then were outlandishly grand and better-looking than anything else we owned.

TJ was even gladder than I was. He hugged Belle around her knees. "I love you," he said, and I envied him the ease with which he said the words. "I'm glad you ain't sick no more." To him, it had all been a sickness, something a person got over, that in all likelihood would never strike again.

Mr. B. fetched home a quarter of butchered beef from the Gundersons. They were feeding a haying crew and in the hot August weather the fresh meat would keep only a short while. It had to be eaten, quick, or canned or salted down for winter. So for three days we feasted on steaks; then Belle decided to make a huge tub of stew, part of which she would can in mason jars. "When we open those jars next winter we'll feel rich as Croesus," she said. I was glad to hear her talk about next winter.

The awful summer had burned up most of the garden, had charred the strawberries, but we were able to salvage a few potatoes and some carrots, the staples of good stew. "You two go out now and collect me some wild onions and rutabagas off the prairie," she ordered. "You won't need to gather many—they're strong enough to take out the tonsils of a grown man—but we can't have a genuine stew without 'em!"

TJ and I skipped straight to the task of doing as she said. I took a kitchen fork from the drawer and TJ fetched a small pail from the barn.

"Ain't it grand, Willie," he said as we trekked east from House Place. "Belle loves us again."

"Oh, I think she always loved us, TJ. She just felt bad inside."

"So did I," he said.

"I know, TJ. We all did. It was a bad time for everybody."

"I thought she might . . . die, Willie."

"TJ, you still got a knack for burying people before their days are numbered."

The wild onions from the prairie were not like ordinary anemic garden onions. Their tops were short, the bulbs amber-colored, and when you took hold of them they perfumed the flesh of your fingers with an odor that didn't wash away for days. When our bucket was a quarter full, I told TJ we had enough to flavor a whole washtub of stew.

We'd taken longer than I intended; our shadows stretched ahead of us like tree trunks as we hiked for home. We hurried, for we knew we were headed to a

House Place filled with the smells of supper and a Belle who smiled again. I got a stitched-together feeling just thinking about it.

TJ saw Belle before I did. "What's she doing, Willie?" he asked. "Coming to meet us? Only why so dressed up?" There wasn't, as yet, alarm in his voice.

Belle had just stepped from House Place. She clutched a small parcel to her chest. She pulled the door shut behind her. She wore her lavender traveling hat; its veil floated about her face like mist. She marched to the spot where the two small grave markers stood side by side, one of them silvered from sun and wind, the other still new and golden. She wrestled them out of the ground, brushed them off, tucked them under her arm.

TJ raised his hand to his mouth and made ready to call to her. I trapped his fingers in my own. "Don't say a word," I ordered.

"Why not?" Suddenly his voice was shivery.

When had I known what was going to happen? Forever, it seemed. Yet all I could say was, "TJ, I got a feeling we fished in this pond before."

Belle strode to the corral; she fussed with the wood and leather latch on the gate. She called the Snowbird to her. She held the mare's silver head against her own red one, while a lavender fog floated above them both. She pulled the Snowbird's ear down and whispered something into it. I could not hear her words but I knew well enough what they were:

If you love something, you set it free. If it comes back to you, it's yours. If it doesn't, it was never meant to be.

Then she turned on her heel and swung the gate open. She stepped aside. The Snowbird lowered her head and her mane cascaded over her neck like a silver waterfall. She began to circle the corral with lissome strides.

"Willie, I think you better . . ."

"Hush, TJ."

The Snowbird trotted past the wide-open gate but

did not exit it the first time. She circled again, then again, picking up speed each time.

At last, with a burst of speed that snatched the breath from my body, she flew through the gate. Her head was high. She lifted her tail as the valedictory banner it was meant to be. Her forelock was lifted away from her brow to show me a pair of astonished morning glory eyes.

I turned to follow her flight: she rose like a soul, pale and free, and floated without a sound over the burnished prairie. Through the wheat field that tomorrow would be harvested by July and Mr. B. Up the incline to that place where three lone pines stood like Sioux warriors against the sky. Then she was gone. I whirled and started to run toward House Place.

Only there was no hatted figure at the corral gate. Then I saw her: far down the empty road, headed east. She had unfurled her yellow organdy parasol; the grave boards were tucked under her arm. She grew smaller and smaller, like a figure you might view through the wrong end of a telescope. In a few hours' time she would be on a train leaving the Territory.

"Come back here!" I shrieked. "*Goddam* you, why'd you ruin everything?" She did not dignify my remarks by so much as turning a hair.

"I hope you *never* find what you're looking for, you *crazy* lady!" I caterwauled at the top of my lungs. "I hope you never get to Morocco or Paris or Port-au-Prince! I wish you were *dead,* Belle Bannerman! Dead, dead, *dead!*"

I pitched myself headlong into the yard. I clawed the ground until my fingernails broke. Tasted dirt in my mouth. Spit out a pebble. I screamed; I cursed; I howled.

When there wasn't another demented holler left in me, I flopped onto my back like a beached bluegill on a Mississippi sandbar. The sky over my head did not reproach me; it was the same prairie sky it'd always been. Except that Belle Bannerman had just sneaked under the edge of it.

TJ stood over me, straining his eyes down the road.

He looked a hundred and ten years old. He raised both hands and made a megaphone. "I hope you find blue butterflies, Aunt Belle," he called. "A whole field of butterflies. . ."

He lowered his gaze to mine. Why had I ever imagined he looked like an elf rescued one twilight from the lilac bush in our front yard? Or that he'd ever had eyes the color of crushed violets? Now those eyes, a pair of hard blue aggies, studied me with disdain.

"Willie, long as I've known you, you been howling about something. Big things. Little things. Always howling. I doubt you ever loved anyone. Including the Snowbird. Something else, too: the fire at the *Tribune was* an accident. Just like Mr. Rich said it was."

"You're crazy. You don't know what you're talking about."

"I saw those three men try to put it out. With my own eyes, Willie. They only wanted to burn up the newsprint Papa kept stacked on the back porch. Didn't aim to burn the whole blamed place down. They tried to stomp it out. One of 'em even took to whacking at it with his jacket. Only the flames got away from him and started up the wall and then it was too late."

"Why didn't you ever tell me? Why pick this particular moment?"

"I tried to tell you, Willie. On the train, for instance. Only you don't listen to nobody, Willie. You never do."

"It wasn't an accident," I insisted. "It couldn't have been. I know what I know."

"Sure you do, Willie. That's all you know, too."

"Did it ever occur to you," I hollered, flat on my back, my words crossing at right angles with his, "that everybody I ever loved got up and left me? Mama and Papa? Miss Pratt? The Snowbird? Belle? Did that ever occur to you? *Huh?*"

But he was through with me. He left me lying right there in the middle of the yard, went into the house, closed the door after himself. I got up, brushed myself off, and followed him.

Belle had left a package on the table. It was

wrapped in a page from a seed catalog. I opened it.
Nestled there was the blue enamel lapel watch and a
note in her wild and spidery script: "For you, Willie,"
she'd written, "so that you never forget what time it
is."

I hurled it across the room. It struck the door and I
heard the crystal break. So much for Papa's notion
about being civilized. Then I climbed the ladder into
the attic, grabbed Papa's valise, and threw it down into
the kitchen ahead of me. I took out my Journal. I
moved the stew to the back of the stove, raised up the
front lid, threw in the blue and burgundy ledger. Next
I upended the valise and out tumbled corners of envelopes, scraps of newsprint, backs of old bills of lading.
They fell into the fire like moths shaken from an old
coat.

I watched the Journal and my scribblings burn.
Tales of love and loss, of which TJ claimed I knew
nothing . . . *descended, that filly was, from a silver
great-grandsire who'd rocketed onto the Western plains
. . . his eyes were like the skies of Finland must be,
pale and clear and cold . . . a blue and yellow scarf
was knotted around her neck and floated behind her
like the wings of a butterfly . . . if envy comes in
colors, they are the blues and greens and roses of sunlight filtered through a piece of stained glass in a rich
man's house . . .* covered with the tracery of my
dreams, the paper curled, turned brown, danced in the
flames, was gone.

Only one thing I could not turn loose of: I had to
believe there'd been a hanging in Tennessee. Otherwise, it was like spitting on my whole life. But whether
there had been or not, the Snowbird never came back.

Nor did I ever lay eyes on Belle Bannerman again.

19

The house Mr. B. rented for us in Red River was painted the color of fresh cow pies. But it was clean and had three rooms and though each of them was small we had more space for ourselves than we'd ever had at House Place. In the kitchen was a small, cripple-legged cookstove. The parlor had a pair of large windows that looked out upon the back door to the Pastime Saloon, which on more than one evening afforded the sort of education Mr. B. would never have wished for me.

The third and smallest room was one in which TJ and I were to sleep. It might've pleased Mrs. Rich to have known that although I did not yet have a room all to myself, at least now I had my own pallet. Just a simple one, laid over a plain pine board. Nearby was a shelf on which I arranged my few treasures: the piece of typeset, the mirror with a broken handle, two books (one of them smoke-damaged).

Mr. B. made a sign and hung it out in front of the house. "Prof. Randall M. Bannerman," it read, "Music Teacher and Theorist."

"Does the *M* stand for Michael?" I asked, thinking of John Michael Bannerman.

"Yes, Willie, it does."

"Who was John, then?"

"Someone Belle knew a long time ago, Willie."

"Oh."

His first student was a girl with thin hair and a nervous hiccup named Mary Martha Milhouse. Mr. B.

also began to write music again. "For your father," he told me, "it was words that tugged at the spirit. For me, it is music. Notes instead of words. The possibilities in their endless arrangements and rearrangement and what they might be made to say to people." It was the longest speech I'd ever heard him make. He could do what he wanted with his music; I, for one, was through forever with words.

Sometimes, in the evening, he played his creations for TJ and me. High, plaintive tunes made more pleading because they were played on a violin, which in my opinion is not the most cheerful of instruments. To me, those tunes spoke only of Belle and everything that I preferred to forget.

When Mr. B. packed up our belongings and prepared to leave House Place—the packing itself did not take long, for there were only a few cooking pots, some blankets, and the brass boat to be loaded into the wagon loaned to us by the Gundersons—July informed us of a decision he said he'd been slow coming to.

"Reckon it's time for me to go home, too," he said.

"You told me once you didn't need a home. Said all you needed was a wagon and Sorry and no worries to dog you," I reminded him.

But he had recanted. "I been too long at the fair, sis. My pa, if he's still living, is an old man now. Ma is dead, gone before I ever left Nebraska. Maybe Pa and me can batch together. Or maybe there's some old gal down there crazy enough to take up with a fella like me."

"I doubt it," I said, "but they say wonders never cease."

"And you remind me of the man who tried to teach a pig to sing. Finally concluded it took too long and annoyed the pig besides."

"Is that a fact?" I pulled on my hair. It was long enough to tie in a knot under my chin. "Sticks and stones, July. Words don't have any effect on me anymore. Besides, why'd you want to get married after what happened to Mr. B.?"

"You're too hard on Belle," he told me.

"She walked out on him. That's a known fact. On TJ and me, too. Merribelle, not to mention John Michael, were Mr. B.'s babies, too. Anybody'd think she hatched 'em all by herself. But Mr. B. didn't take off on us like a kite in a high wind. Only That One." I thought of her mostly as That One. She had ceased to be a person to me.

"Sis, when you go to dig a grave for an enemy, remember to dig two."

"Don't fill me up with that kind of stuff," I said. "I know what I know. That One was mean and selfish. I hope we never lay eyes on her again."

"And I think I'll learn to thank my stars there's too many miles between here and Nebraska for you to visit too often." Our conversations were as familiar as roads we'd walked down before.

July was ready to pull out of the yard at the same time we were. Mr. B. did not know how to manage the farewell. His pale, thin hands dangled at his sides. It was left to July to hold out a perennially soiled mitt and to seize one of Mr. B.'s limp ones. He clapped another hand on top of the one he gripped.

"You always been a fair man to me," July told him, "a good man who tried hard. Can't nobody ask better of another."

Mr. B.'s eyes were glisteny. He lurched forward and hugged July in a way that made me suspect he hadn't practiced it often. But he couldn't bring himself to say the words: *Good-bye. Take care of yourself. See you around.*

"Come and visit us in Red River," TJ invited grandly. "We got lots of room there. You could even sleep in the house."

July reached out to ruffle my brother's hair. "Sure, Thomas. I just might do that," all of us knowing he never would. TJ beamed. *Thomas.* Since I had to call him Thomas he didn't seem like my brother anymore. I thought TJ in my head but had to put Thomas on my tongue. Otherwise, he wouldn't answer me.

"Good-bye, sis," July said to me. He did not ruffle my hair. I am not, of course, a person who invites

hair-ruffling. Nevertheless, on that particular occasion,
I might have accepted some token gesture. He gave me
none.

"You aim to send us a letter to let us know you got
to Nebraska all right?" I wanted to know. There was
that tingling under the bridge of my nose.

"Don't worry 'bout me, sis. I remember the way.
And I sure hope these two unfortunate fellas don't
starve on your cooking."

"Good-bye," I said. Enough was enough.

"Good-bye, sis. Keep the tail on the hide." He
pulled out of the yard and headed southeast. We went
north into Red River. I looked back once: July was
looking back at me. He raised five splayed fingers
against the sky in a farewell salute. He had not even
been kin, but I had loved him more than if he had
been. I wanted to call it out: *I love you, July Chemeliewski*. But I did nothing of the sort. It was not my
style.

When we were settled, Mr. B. made us breakfast every morning and I got supper every night. I learned to
make baking powder biscuits, blueberry grunt, and
stew that was almost as good as Belle's. Every evening
Thomas went out to play and Mr. B. gave his music
lessons. I finally stopped saying ain't.

"Are you really a professor?" I asked Mr. B. one
day. I don't know why I doubted it, but I did.

"I was once. Before I met Belle. Perhaps it was
something I ought never to have given up. That might
have been one of my many mistakes."

"You didn't make many," I said. "Your main problem was That One hankering after impossibles. Avocadoes and persimmons. Strawberries big as pullet eggs.
A baby, when maybe one was never meant to be. If
she'd been different, you'd still be a professor."

"Willie, no matter how thin you make the pancake,
it always has two sides."

"Don't defend her," I yelped. "She don't deserve it."

"Of course she does, Willie."

"She ruined our lives. Ruined mine, at any rate."

"You're the one doing that, Willie."

"She was plain old cat-crazy, that's what. Where'd you ever meet up with a person like her, anyhow?"

"Belle was a singer."

A singer? I remembered how she sang. "Where in the world did she sing, with a voice like hers?"

"It was at a place . . . rather like the Pastime."

"Oh." No one ever understood how she came to marry a man like your uncle, Mr. Rich had said. She was unusual; a most unusual woman. What he meant was she was brassy and sassy and full of warm color—all the things Mr. B. had loved.

We received a single postcard from her. The postmark was smudged and we could not make it out. There was no return address on the card and I knew there was never meant to be. The picture on it was of an orange grove close beside a sea with a beach of white sand. Her handwriting was cramped: "Yesterday I came upon a field of blue butterflies. I caught some in my bonnet and they were lovely as a hatful of dreams." She had not signed her name.

Thomas scrutinized the postmark a long time. "I think it says Port-au-Prince," he decided.

I looked, too. "It's too smudged to tell for sure, Thomas."

He looked away, out the window that viewed the back entry of the Pastime. "No," he allowed, "I am sure that it says Port-au-Prince. She has found that place she wanted to be." He would not surrender the card to me or Mr. B. He kept it under his pillow, and the last time I chanced to see it, it had been worn thin and limp from being looked at so often.

One night Mr. B. fetched the new schoolteacher home for supper. "Willie, I want you to meet Mr. Foster. He will take over where Miss Pratt left off. It will mean you and Thomas can go back to school again."

I gave Mr. Foster a slave trader's sizing up as I cut a batch of biscuits. At least he was taller than I was. His hair was crinkly and yellow, and as male persons go, not the worst-looking specimen I'd ever seen. "You know anything about John Keats?" I demanded sternly.

" 'But this is human life: the war, the deeds,
The disappointment, the anxiety . . .
All human; bearing in themselves this good,
That they are still the air, the subtle food,
To make us feel existence, and to show
How quiet death is.'
Endymion, Book II," he stammered.

"Well," I allowed, "the biscuits will be ready in a minute. I guess you'll do in a pinch." As though I were responsible for hiring and paying him myself.

"Perhaps we can read some poetry together sometime," he said.

"I doubt it. I've sworn off that sort of thing."

For of course a day did not pass but what I thought about the Snowbird. Most often she came to me at night: in that floaty time between waking and sleeping she would appear against the starry curtain of my dreams, a silver phantom now whole and perfect and in no manner tarnished by the ordeal I had forced her through. I longed, however, for a time when I would not think of her at all. Wondered if it might not be better if I would someday stumble across her bones, bleached white upon the prairie, and know that she was truly gone. I longed, too, for a way to put the past behind me, where it belonged.

"You want to come with me, Thomas?" I suggested one afternoon. Together we would go back to House Place; we could make proper and ceremonial goodbyes; I would tie up my odds and ends like I ought to've done long since.

"Why would I want to go out there, Willie? Lordy—what's out there to see? An empty old house. A barn with no horses in it. Even the chickens are gone. July, too." July would have been tickled to hear himself ranked right along with a few speckled chickens.

"Then I'll go alone."

"So go. Everything I like is right here in Red River." It was true: he'd made a regular gaggle of friends; some of them even called him Tommy. It was a name I detested even more than Thomas. Why couldn't he have gone on being TJ forever?

"Forget I asked. No skin off this old nose if you don't want to tag along. I got no strings on you."

"Sure don't."

"I said, forget I asked."

"I forgot already." With that, he was out the door and off to play. I stuffed a cold biscuit and an apple in my pocket and left him where he belonged. It sure hadn't taken him long to get the hang of city living.

20

I walked back to House Place across the random, left-over land that had so surprised my eyes a November morning one hundred years before. Only it hadn't been a hundred. Only two. Twenty-four months. I'd been thirteen then. Now I was past fifteen. Wasn't any prettier; no fatter; hardly any wiser. Only difference was now I had hair.

This time, though, I could see House Place from a long way off because I knew what to look for: a low, disheveled dwelling fashioned of sod, tar paper, and logs emerging from a low-sloping creekside. It winked at me with a south-facing eye. When I got closer, I could see that it looked as ruined and lonesome as I felt.

I walked to the door and stopped. Did I really want to do what I was about to do? I took the latch in my hand and the door swung open of its own accord.

Herschvogel sat silently in the middle of the room. Sam Elliott, who owned the Pastime and was soon to be married, had purchased Herschvogel from Mr. B. but had not yet come to fetch him to a new home in Red River. I sat down on a nail keg chair. A low-flying bird had broken one of the panes from the window near where we'd eaten all our meals, played our games of blackjack. Ground squirrels had gnawed the doorsill to shreds. Pages of the *Saturday Evening Post,* applied shortly before the departure of That One, now hung in graceful streamers from the wall.

I threw back my head and let out a mournful howl.

"Give it all back, Somebody!" I cried. "Make me a present of the smell of coffee in a pot of robin's egg blue! Let me hear the whisper of cards from a game played on a winter night a million years ago! And Somebody, Somebody—bring me back a horse the color of snow!"

Nothing happened, of course. Herschvogel did not magically find a tongue with which to lecture me. The walls of House Place did not sprout arms to fold around me. The only sound in my ears was the faded ticking of my own heart; the only smell one of ruin and decay.

I got up from the nail keg chair. I brushed pieces of broken glass into a tidy pile with my foot. Swept mouse commas off Herschvogel's back. Picked five fat dust mice off the floor. Walked to the door, stepped through it, let it swing shut behind me. What was it, anyhow, the thing I was looking for? Would I recognize it when it came my way? Questions without answers. Lordy, Lordy! I'd asked 'em my whole life long. It was a hard habit to break.

The corral gate languished half-open, as we'd carelessly left it the day we moved into Red River. I went to straighten it, set it aright, latch it one final time. There, held securely by the latch hook, where That One left it, knowing I would be back someday, was the silver wishing ring.

I tried to slide it onto my ring finger . . . *wise, old, sensible Willie; older, my girl, than I'll ever be! . . . she never asked, then or later, why I chose to mutilate myself in such a way . . . eyes as fierce and clever as those of a fox, but filled with such uncommon sweetness when she smiled* . . . the ring wouldn't fit. Already my hands were bigger than hers would ever be. I moved the ring to my little finger; there it was too large.

As carefully as I had woven them together in the first place, I separated each strand from its companions. I held the crinkled silver hairs in my palm. An autumn wind rose up. Somewhere a meadowlark called my name: *Wil-eeee, Wil-eeee.* One by one by one, I lifted the silver strands, carriers of dreams, and let the wind take them across the prairie where they belonged. *If you love a thing, you set it free. If it comes back to you, it's yours.*

That One had taken the moss agates with her when she left, even the ones Thomas and I had collected. Each had preserved in its depths a vision as timeless as a moonscape: immobile trees, unscalable cliffs, tawny meadows fixed forever in silica and quartz. Never in this life could they be altered or made ugly. And there was a way to keep the Snowbird with me a whole life long. . . .

I ran back to Red River as fast as a pair of lanky shanks could carry me. I hooted. Leaped up to catch a handful of blue October sky. *If it comes back to you, it's yours.* Why had I worried about marching left when everyone else was marching right? Or if I would always be up my own tree, alone? Now it did not seem such a terrible way to be. Why, I might soon even consider reading a bit of Keats with Mr. Foster!

The house in Red River seemed deserted when I rushed into it. Then, from the parlor, came the caught-the-cat's-tail-in-the-door sound of Mary Martha Milhouse trying to coax a civilized racket out of Mr. B.'s violin. Outside, Thomas cried, *Ollie, Ollie oxen free.*

I opened Papa's valise. I removed the new copybook Mr. B. had gotten for me. I took out the blue enamel lapel watch. Beneath the cracked crystal its numerals were garlanded by pink rosebuds and entwined by tiny green leaves. I knew what time it was.

After all, my ancestors had carried a king's colors into battle. I was descended from the likes of James Robertson, and my kinswoman had dared to wear the uniform of a Union major during the Civil War. More than that, I was the only daughter of two people who had believed in dreaming and telling.

I began to write.

The Snowbird rose like a soul, pale and serene, and floated without a sound across the burnished prairie of my mind. Her mane and tail were unfurled silver banners, her eyes a pair of astonished morning glories. Someday, I hoped, in far-off Morocco or Paris or Port-au-Prince, That One might read my tale and hear me call across time and space:

I love you, too, Belle Bannerman, and I hope you've located that place not to be found on any map. Then, the tracery of my dreams appeared on the white page before me, round and firm and accountable:

THE SNOWBIRD

by

Willanna Bannerman,

TERRITORY OF DAKOTA, 1885

White horses occupy a special niche in the recorded facts and fables of human history . . . The most famous white horse on the American frontier was called The Pacing White Mustang or The Ghost Horse of the Prairie. Washington Irving wrote in 1822 that this horse "could rack [pace] faster than the fastest steed can run." In 1830, Josiah Gregg, a famous newspaper reporter, described an animal that was "medium-sized and milk-white, save for a pair of black-tipped ears," and in 1851, Herman Melville wrote that this "magnificent white charger trooped westward like a chosen star." When last seen in 1887, The Ghost Horse of the Prairie was running wild and free in the Snake River region of Idaho. . . .

ABOUT THE AUTHOR

PATRICIA CALVERT, who lives in Chatfield, Minnesota, is a senior editorial assistant in the Section of Publications of the Mayo Clinic. She holds a degree in history and is working on a master's degree in children's literature. She is the author of numerous stories and articles published for young readers. THE SNOWBIRD is her first novel.